WOLF JOURNAL

WOLF JOURNAL

a novel

Brian A. Connolly

Library of Congress Number: 2001119575
ISBN #:   Hardcover   1-4010-3864-6
                 Softcover   1-4010-3863-8

This novel is a work of fiction. The characters and events are products of the author's imagination. Any similarity to real people and events is coincidental.

Aldo Leopold quote: From A SAND COUNTY ALMANAC: AND SKETCHES HERE AND THERE by Aldo Leopold, copyright 1945, 1977 by Oxford University Press, Inc. Used by permission of Oxford University Press, Inc.

Cover Photograph: *The Druid Peak Pack*, copyright 1997 by Dan and Cindy Hartman. Used by permission. Courtesy of Wildlife Along the Rockies Gallery, Silver Gate, Montana.

Author photo by Patricia Chalmers.

This book was printed in the United States of America.

To order additional copies of this book, contact:
Xlibris Corporation
1-888-7-XLIBRIS
www.Xlibris.com
Orders@Xlibris.com

For Nathan and Heather
who love things wild
and
The Druid Peak Pack of Yellowstone
whose inspiration is the heart of *Wolf Journal*

In memory of:
Joe, Alyce, Peter and Sharon Connolly
and
Dennis J. Hannan

Acknowledgements:

Special thanks to Ray & Darlene Rathmell of Lock Haven, Pennsylvania for sharing their fly fishing expertise over campfires in Wyoming; to John Uhler (The Total Yellowstone Page) for his dedication to all things wild and for his wonderful sense of humor; to former students Nicole Monforti and Josh Wynn for their insightful reading of the manuscript; to the RCK English Faculty for caring so much; to Judy Connolly, Kathy & Kate Reynolds whose advice and encouragement always came in equal portions; to poet and painter Robert Adam for his long friendship and for teaching me the power of words; to the park rangers at Isle Royale and Yellowstone for sharing their wolf wisdom; to Nathan Connolly for his confidence in my work; to Heather Connolly for her energetic reading of the manuscript and for her keen eye for details; to the late Dennis Hannan for his gentle hand on all those 'things that intrude on my reading pleasure'.

Author's Note:

In July of 1997, I spent two cold nights and three freezing mornings standing near the confluence of Soda Butte Creek and the Lamar River in Yellowstone hoping to get a glimpse of one of the wolves released there during the 1995-96 reintroduction program. The early morning temperatures were near freezing. The valley is approximately 7000 feet above sea level with mountains rising another 2500 feet on either side. The valley is open rangeland with dried grasses and sagebrush, excellent for spotting wildlife. The mountains are partially forested with Douglas fir and aspen, and, above tree line, rock cliffs are exposed.

With a few others, I waited and waited. We saw a golden eagle, a bald eagle, several ravens, a black bear, a small herd of bison, and a few elk and pronghorn antelope. Even several coyotes. But no sign of a wolf. Down by the streams, Sand Hill Cranes called in raspy voices. Along the water's edge, river otters played slippery games.

On the morning of the third day I arrived at four a.m. This was to be my last day in the park. Several people joined me by five a. m. I had been standing still for two hours watching my breath hang in the frozen air when I heard the first howl. It came from the thick pines at the base of Druid Peak where biologists had located a den site. That first howl, long and mournful, was joined by a second, a third, then two or three more. Their songs filled the forest like a choir in a great cathedral. The howling continued for fifteen minutes followed by five minutes of silence. Then a wolf appeared on the ridge above us several hundred yards away. She was gray with some brown and white, approximately eighty-five pounds. She walked among the dried grasses and sagebrush to a sunny spot where she stretched out on her side. Soon she was joined by four pups, three grays and a black, each twenty-five pounds having been born in April. They leapt on her and each other; bit tails and ears, and fought over sticks and pinecones.

I was overwhelmed. I had spent a lot of time in wild places, but never thought I'd see anything like this. There was nothing between those wolves and me except wildflowers. Even though tears were welling up, I couldn't stop smiling. I stayed in the park ten more days. Since that morning I have logged several hundred sightings each time wondering how it would be if the wolves I was seeing were in the Allegheny Mountains of Pennsylvania where I grew up.

Every summer now I camp at Pebble Creek in the Lamar Valley. It was in a tent there where much of this novel was written. Even though the story has no direct connection to the Yellowstone wolves, *Wolf Journal* is my reaction to that frozen morning when I saw my first wolf in the wild.

BAConnolly
Bend, Oregon

We reached the old wolf in time to watch a fierce green fire dying in her eyes. I realized then, and have known ever since, that there was something new to me in those eyes-something known only to her and to the mountain.

Aldo Leopold from 'Thinking like a Mountain'
A Sand County Almanac: and Sketches Here and There, 1945

1

The full moon colors the mist in the dark woods a pale yellow. Shadows move slowly along the creek bank, a wolf pack, two gray adults with five pups, their first hunt. Their undulating reflections brush against the moon floating in a deep pool below rapids. The alpha male reads the wind, inhales a familiar scent and bolts up the hillside. His mate leaps over rocks to follow him. The pups, almost as large as their parents, scramble in a disorganized line behind her. Their breathing is heavy, tongues lolling as they crest the mountaintop. Intermittently, each body is bathed in moonlight, a long line of silvery predators, muscles flexing under thick fur with every stride.

Ahead, an injured whitetail limps along a trail. The deer whirls around in a circle too confused by the rush of the pack to take flight. As the moon follows its well-worn path across the sky, the wolves feed. When the first stain of light appears, a single stroke across the eastern sky, the alpha male begins to howl, long, low notes like a mournful wind gradually rising then trailing off. The pups and the female join in, each voice, separated by a subtle octave, singing the same plaintive notes.

The song of the wolf is among the most beautiful sounds in nature. The lonesome howl, the excited yaps and barks, the intimidating growl all symbolize wilderness. My father says the only true wilderness is one in which the entire food chain is intact. He says because the wolf has been exterminated in Pennsylvania, there is no wilderness left in our state. "A forest without the wolf," he said, "is just a big park."

It has been a hundred years since the wild wolf's voice has been heard in the Allegheny Mountains. According to Hawk, an Indian friend of mine, a dozen wolf packs once roamed the upper Allegheny valley north and south of our village. His people, the Susquehannocks, told stories about how wolves would sing them to sleep when they were gathered around the fire in their winter lodges. Once asleep, the wolves would speak to them in dream. Hawk's ancestors understood wolf and came to know their hunt stories, reunion stories and birth stories.

One of the stories was the *Going Away Tale* that was about the death of a great wolf. He was the largest wolf in the valley and led a pack of twenty animals. The Indians knew this wolf as Shadow because he was all black. According to the wolves who sang his tale, Shadow was a supreme hunter, a brave leader, a loyal mate and a protective parent. He was known to run over these mountains as much as forty miles in a day leading the pack to elk and buffalo which also lived in our valley during the last century.

Shadow's story mostly focused on his going away, his death. When he was very old, he was kicked by an elk. Shadow wandered off alone into the deep woods to die. The other wolves could hear his death song coming from a distant ridge between two hills. His howls, however, were not of despair, but of joy and hope. The lyrics spoke of the many gifts with which Shadow had been blessed. One by one he called the individual names of his pack distributing strength to this one, cunning to that one, honor to a third, understanding to a fourth, stamina to another, courage to a young one and so on. In his going away, Shadow had given himself back to the pack. By sunrise his song ceased.

In the valley a howl began. At first one voice sang out, then two, then five more until the entire pack called to the morning sky. The chorus, heard as if from some ancient cathedral, was not a call to hunt or a cry of loss, but was a sincere tribute to their lost leader.

The Indians say that the legend of Shadow explains to them why wolves live and hunt cooperatively. Each has his own talent to add to the strength of the family, the pack. Hawk's ancestral tribe believed the dream stories revealed to them important truths about how to conduct their own lives. That is why they followed the way of the wolf and, to this day, honor its spirit in their art and dance.

2

*A*aron raised his hand. The class was silent.

"Yes, Aaron?" said Mr. Fletcher, his slim English teacher.

"So, what you're saying is that we should keep a weekly journal on any topic we choose. Like I could do dirt bikes or fishing or girls!" He raised both eyebrows and smiled at Sara.

"Right, Aaron, although you may wish to wait a few years before you write about girls." Several boys snickered.

"We'll never have that much to say on one topic, Mr. Fletcher," said Sara tossing her red curls.

"You'll have plenty to say if you pick the right subject. It must be something you are really interested in, something you are really passionate about other than the opposite sex." Mr. Fletcher looked at Aaron. "All of our journal entries since September have been about different subjects. However, a page or two about something hasn't allowed us to go into depth. This topic approach will help us avoid shallowness in our writing and thinking, help us to really explore something that is important to us.

"There is a girl right in this class who can talk all day and all night about computers. There is a person here who not only fly fishes, but ties her own flies and sells them. In order to do that, she has to understand the life cycles of many insects, the feeding habits of trout as well as which colors and patterns most effectively mimic bugs. We have a classmate who has won gold medals at the state and national level in archery, another girl with a black belt, a boy who can do back flips off a jump with his snowboard and a boy who knows a lot about organic crop farming. There is a girl in my afternoon class who sews pieces of cloth together to create beautiful quilts each of which tells a story from her family history. In that same class is another girl who has a fine collection of spiders and snakes. For ninth graders, you are amazing people.

"Now, to help you discover what you are most interested in, number to ten on your paper. List ten specific things you like. Don't write animals. That's too general. Write wolf."

Jimmy looked up, his eyes wide. He had already written wolf down. He wondered if Mr. Fletcher knew his secret.

"I can only think of five things," Ricky called out from the back of the room.

Susan whispered, "Put down after school detention."

"Not funny," said Ricky.

Mr. Fletcher asked, "Did you list music, art, cars, fishing, running, tennis, cooking, baseball cards or magic? What about juggling? Once you have your list complete, circle the best topic for you."

The teacher paced up and down the rows of desks inspecting lists, making suggestions. "Jimmy, you only have one thing on your list," he said.

"I know," said Jimmy. "It's what I want to write about."

"I'll make you a deal," Mr. Fletcher said, "if after you write down nine more topics, you still want to do wolves, you can do it. A deal?"

"A deal," Jimmy said.

Mr. Fletcher continued to the class, "Now, in this journal you will be going into great depth. You'll be including a lot of facts about your subject, but what I really want is for you to go beyond facts. Explore why you're so excited about the subject you've chosen. What is it that draws you to it; what is the source of that power? Does your subject ignite your imagination and, if so, where does that imagination take you?

"For example, if you are writing about dance, ballet or modern, what do you see when you close your eyes and think about being on stage? What music is playing? How does it feel to be graceful? What do you communicate to the audience when you move a certain way? How is your dancing like painting or sculpture or playing the violin?"

Jimmy looked up the next row at Sherry. Her corn silk hair curled about her shoulders catching light the way a waterfall does in the early morning sun. As if she could feel his eyes on her, she turned and looked at him. He turned away quickly feeling a flush come to his face. To cover his embarrassment, Jimmy raised his hand. "I wrote down ten things and I still want to do wolves. Is that okay?"

"Yes, Jimmy," said Mr. Fletcher.

"Hey, Jimmy," said Big Charlie, "my dad says that wolves are devils. The best kind is one that's been shot through the head!" He laughed.

Fletcher gave him a look. "Your father isn't writing a journal! Let me see your list, Charles. Very good: ballet, sewing, cooking pastries." Everyone except Big Charlie laughed.

"That's not what I wrote," he muttered.

Fletcher said, "See, Charles, it's not nice to make fun of someone else's topic." Big Charlie's face darkened and he brooded over his paper.

Jimmy said, "It's okay, Mr. Fletcher. I don't pay him no mind. Would it be okay if we drew some pictures in our journal to illustrate what we are writing about?" He had already started a sketch of a wolf running through a forest.

"That's fine as long as your entries have a few pages of writing. Remember, writing is ultimately what journal writing aims to improve."

"Oh, Mr. Fletcher," Jimmy continued, " I have a journal at home that I made last summer. It doesn't have any writing in it yet. Could I use that one?"

"What do you mean 'you made'?" said Fletcher.

"Well, I just made the cover. My mom cut paper and sewed it in so I could draw and write. It's the same size as a regular old composition book."

Fletcher said, "I think the more personalized your journal is, the better. Go ahead, use it."

Jimmy's imagination had already begun to bloom. The classroom sounds diminished as if a volume control was being turned down until everything was just a whisper. The soundtrack in Jimmy's head grew in intensity as the movie that he watched there came into focus. Wind sweeping through the woods near the head of Two Mile Creek caused leafless trees to creak and crowded branches to drum against one another. Snow blew around the head of the valley settling in soft humps over rock or in long drift ridges north of each tree trunk creating a white sculptured garden through which Jimmy hiked.

The late afternoon light was thin. The sky was in the woods which meant from this point on it was all downhill to the farm on Lillibridge Creek. Jimmy scanned the dark tree trunks for woodpeckers, branches for hawks, owls or roosting turkeys. He watched the far woods for whitetail deer and surveyed the ground nearby for tracks of any kind. He loved the stories the woods told him: the place where the buck rubbed velvet from his antlers, the dense berry patch where quail fed, the drama of hoof and wing and paw played out in creek mud or in newly fallen snow. Well those tracks he read as if they were words printed on a line across a white page.

The best tracking was when he found a new print, one with which he was not familiar or a variation of one he thought he knew. It had been like that the previous spring when he found the mink tracks along the creek near the barn. He had thought otter, then fisher, but something wasn't quite right about those choices. In his notebook he wrote date, time, location, mud conditions and rejected choices. He drew the tracks in intricate detail across the margins so that he could have the design of each track as well as the paired pattern they made which was always an important clue to solving the mystery of identification. He also recorded the distance between tracks and the depth of each, indicators of size and weight depending on mud consistency. Later,

Jimmy discovered that his drawings matched the mink tracks in his field guide. The dark, sleek critters hadn't been seen in the valley for many years. This was a real find, which he kept a secret to protect the animals from local trappers.

In his daydream, Jimmy crossed Two Mile Creek and followed a deer run through a stand of birch to a cluster of white pines. Their wide branches floated like green clouds against the gray sky, a stark contrast to the dull winter colors that surrounded them.

Where there was just a dusting of snow under the pines, Jimmy rested. The circles of exposed ground covered with wheat colored pine needles told him that deer had bedded down there earlier in the day, three adults and a yearling. Pinecone scales spread about on the snow indicated squirrels living in these trees.

He picked up a soft, gray owl pellet, which resembled a pussy willow bud, and broke it open. Inside, the skeletal remains of a field mouse, tiny foot and leg bones, a hip joint, a skull. The life and death struggle played itself out in his head: the silent beating of owl wings, the mouse scream, the closing talons. The light snow in the dark woods.

There were many trails that led out from the pines. Jimmy took the one that headed most directly toward the farm. He hadn't gone more than a hundred yards when he came upon another intersecting trail with fresh tracks he did not recognize. He had run into wild dogs along this ridge before, but none had ever left tracks this big. Dogs always traveled in pairs or small groups. This was a single individual. Jimmy knew, too, that a full-grown coyote track might measure two and a half inches in length. These tracks, however, were almost twice that long.

Jimmy was sketching in his notebook one paw print per page when the bell rang signaling the end of English class. The problem with school, he thought, was that it kept interrupting him, pulling him back out of his imagination, which is really where he wanted to spend the rest of the day. There was a whole world of mystery there waiting to be explored. Instead, he had to go to history class and learn about a bunch of civilizations whose tracks had been erased years ago.

3

wj 28 January

On our farm my sisters and I help my parents with all the chores in order to make the farm work successfully. Each has his own responsibilities. Each member of the family contributes to the success of the farm, which is our livelihood.

The same is true for wolves. They live, hunt and raise young in a family pack. There is a strict social order within the pack, which adds to its efficiency and success. There is an adult breeding pair, the alpha male and alpha female. Other adult wolves in the pack are usually offspring of the alpha pair. However, sometimes wolves from other packs will be permitted to join the family. Adult pack members participate together in the hunt. This is important because wolves usually take animals many times their own size. All pack members help raise new pups.

When a pack becomes too large to feed itself, the older male offspring leave to join another pack or find a new territory and start their own family group. Some have been known to wander hundreds of miles from their original location in order to find a mate and begin a new life.

This is what I think happened with the Two Mile wolf. (Remember, Mr. Fletcher, you said to use our imaginations in these journal entries!) While hiking up at the head of the creek, I came across a trail in the snow. Now everyone knows that a track in the snow tends to be larger than one in soft ground, but this canine track was five inches long. If I measure from the bottom of the palm of my hand, my first knuckle is five inches from it. That is a large print! And that does not even include the claw marks! So it's not a coyote or a fox. It could be a wild dog, but the dog would have to be immense. Maybe an Alaskan malamute might leave a big enough track, but I don't know of anyone in the valley who has such a dog.

I talked to Hawk who knows about these things. He called McCleary in Kane who keeps a pack of wolves there for tourists to see. I've seen them several times myself. They are the ones that inspired me to keep this journal. Hawk asked if he was missing any of his captive lobos, but he wasn't. Hawk said that in order for the track I found to belong to a wolf, he would have to have come from Canada five hundred miles away. He said he rode a horse once almost a hundred miles to meet a young girl from another tribe. That may be what my wolf is doing, looking for a mate or a new territory. I suggested to Hawk that this wolf might be the offspring of a wolf that started south some years ago. He said, "Maybe."

From the size and depth of the print in the snow, I estimate the weight of the wolf to be around a hundred and thirty pounds. This means that it's a male. Females are usually smaller. Hawk says that some Alaskan wolves are over a hundred and fifty pounds. Whew! That's bigger than me!

Gray wolves can be white, brown, gray, black or a mix of those colors. I think that the Two Mile wolf is black because that is the only color fur I found on thorns along the trail. So my wolf is a large, black male searching for a mate. Even though I haven't seen him yet, I'll name him Romeo. Hawk says Romeo is looking in the wrong place for a mate. The last sighting of a wolf along the Allegheny River was in the late 1800's, almost a hundred years ago. That wolf was shot not far from where I found Romeo's tracks. It was mounted and can still be seen in the lobby of the county courthouse. It is a black wolf.

4

*J*immy moved along the steep road noiselessly. Several inches of new snow muffled his footsteps. It was an hour before daylight. Plenty of time for him to get into position near the trail he had discovered the previous weekend. Against the white floor of the forest, the birch, maple and oak trees looked like leafless shadows. Above, countless stars shimmered in the clear sky. The clouds had moved east.

The temperature was dropping. It had been twenty when he started hiking at four o'clock. Now it was closer to zero. However, Jimmy had already loosened his jacket. Soon he would remove it, then his sweater, then the wool shirt. Hawk had taught him to dress in layers. Remove layers as the body heats up; add as it cools. This method helps avoid overheating when hiking in the winter. It also keeps away the chills that could lead to hypothermia, a lowering of the body temperature that can take the life of anyone not prepared for prolonged cold weather.

In his backpack, along with his journal and binoculars, was an ample supply of food: apples, corn muffins, thermos of tea and a thermos of venison stoup, a word his mother had coined for her stew-soup recipe. He also carried first aid stuff including a snakebite kit, which he wouldn't need in this cold. The compass he used to orient his drawings to the north. On each page of his journal where a sketch occurred, he drew a compass reading. In a pocket of his backpack next to a band aid box full of matches was Jimmy's hunting knife. During hunting season he used it to field dress deer, squirrel or rabbit. During fishing season he filleted trout. On winter forays into the deep woods he used his knife to create wood shavings for kindling or to whittle sticks, which is what he often did to occupy himself while waiting in one spot for birds and animals to emerge from their hiding places.

As Jimmy made his way up the logging road, the conversation at dinner the night before came back to him. Hawk was there, as was his mother, father, sisters and Lewis, the hired man, who at seventy still did the work of two men. Amidst the aroma of meatloaf, mashed potatoes and corn, words flew like birds. Silverware rattled and scraped. Glasses bumped plates. The fire in the woodstove hissed and snapped.

There was talk of crops and cattle, broken tractors and fences in need of mending. Lewis complained about the government meddling in farmers' affairs. Martha, Jimmy's mother, asked the three kids about school. The girls didn't say much.

Maureen, already in seventh grade, said, "Some friends said that Jimmy has a crush on Sherry Woolman!"

"Who said that?" Jimmy demanded. "It's not so!" His face reddened.

Martha passed the peas to Lewis and said without looking at Jimmy, "Isn't she that nice, young girl from town whose father works for the state or something? I think I met her mother once at a church supper. Very down to earth if you ask me." She forced herself not to smile, but she knew talk about girls made her son uneasy.

Jimmy shrugged and changed the subject. He told them about his wolf journal, the tracks he'd found and the hike he'd be taking in the morning back over the hill to Two Mile Creek.

Jimmy's father, Joe, laughed. "I think you live too much in your imagination," he said. "If what you found really was wolf tracks, they'd be a hundred years old!" Everyone laughed except Hawk.

Hawk's face was a roadmap of wrinkles, his gray hair a long braid down his back, his eyes bright, shinning, alive. He spoke, "The tracks were in snow. Jimmy's eye is good. He draws things that are true. We all know that. I think he will find his wolf if he knows how to wait."

"I know how," said Jimmy.

"When you get to the head of the creek," Hawk continued, "gather firewood, enough for one day. Also, cut some fresh pine boughs. Keep your fire small. It isn't a fire for warming; it is the spiritual fire of the smoke ceremony. Add pine boughs when the fire is healthy. This will give good smoke. Sit near the fire and guide the smoke over your body, over your face and head like so." Hawk gestured with both hands as if pulling smoke toward himself. His old hands moved up his face and over his head. His eyes were closed.

Hawk said, "There are words you can say, but it is better if you find your own words. Your mouth will help you find them. Words that come from inside your own self, ones that aren't born of the ear, but begin life in your heart have more power. Do this 'til daylight fails. It may help you find the wolf. Actually, he will find you."

"Hawk, you old windbag," said Lewis, "you aughten fill this boy's head with such foolishness. His head is already crowded with dreams of things that don't exist."

"My friend, Lewis, may I remind you that my wind is not as old as yours!"

Everyone laughed. Lewis even smiled.

Lewis said, "I love it when I remember things, and I finally recall that guy you were talking about, Martha. Fred Woolman is a ranger, forest ranger. He goes by the book. He fined me fifty dollars some years back just for having a slew of trout in my creel out of season. He let me keep the fish though. A fair enough man if anyone was to ask me."

Sally, Jimmy's ten-year-old sister, said with her mouth full of mashed potatoes, "Who's Fred Woolmouth?"

"Woolman," Lewis corrected her and smiled. "He's the father of that pretty little girlfriend of Jimmy's."

As he trudged through the snow that dark morning, Jimmy thought about Hawk's words. Even though he doubted the value of the smoke ceremony, he would try it. What he did know from his own experience was that sitting still for a long time allowed him to see many things that others missed. Earlier in the winter, on a Saturday morning like this one, Jimmy had seen a Great Horned Owl glide from a thick pine on wings silent as thought. It landed at the base of a boulder where a snowshoe rabbit was feeding on tree bark. There was a brief struggle. Snow erupted like an explosion. Rabbit cries were audible in the quiet morning air. Then, carrying the limp body in his talons, the phantom bird returned to the pine and began to feed.

Jimmy had drawn all over his journal that morning laying out from different angles the whole unfolding story including very detailed likenesses of both characters and the panoramic stage where this drama had taken place.

As he neared the crest of the hill where the logging road cut south, Jimmy thought to himself that the reason he loved these mountains so much was that the forest was a book full of stories. He wanted to read them all. There were stories of the hunt, stories of survival, some touched by humor or beauty and grace, others harsh as death. The stories he liked best were those that contained mystery. The tracks he found last week began such a story. He was back now to read more.

Ahead lay the white pines near which he had found the tracks. Jimmy stood still for a long time evaluating the scene trying to determine the best place to build a fire. He picked a sheltered spot where the wind would carry his human scent north and he'd have a good view looking off toward the creek. The tracks had come from the south, he thought, and if this wolf or dog, this Romeo had established a territory, he just might come through here again.

He knew that the best time to see activity in the woods was just before dark and just after sun up. The thick woods around him had already begun to take on light. Stars had begun to fade. Whole constellations had been snuffed out. Jimmy put on his wool shirt and his green sweater. He watched the foggy patches of his breath rise like smoke signals in the frigid air. He sniffed and listened. He could smell pine scent and a hint of deer musk. There were no sounds. All was still.

The old Allegheny Mountains gradually gave up their secrets. Sunlight brought color to the landscape. Gray trunks of dead trees were partially covered with emerald green moss. The white bellies of halfmoon fungus were visible beneath their snowy shelf. The dark green pine boughs drooped beneath fresh snow. The dense bushes of mountain laurel held olive leaves out to the sun's light. Above the forest the distant blue skin of the sky stretched south like a calm sea.

Rabbits and squirrels moved cautiously in the snow. Blue jays and chickadees called and flitted from branch to branch. The jays caused small avalanches to crash from the pine boughs. The gray and white chickadees hung upside down while foraging for seeds in the brush.

He gathered a substantial store of firewood, sticks mostly, dry as bleached finger bones. He mounded dead leaves above which he built a teepee of small branches. The leaves ignited easily causing a thin stream of gray-blue smoke to curl skyward. The kindling caught fire. Jimmy added larger pieces. Yellow flames danced in the icy air. Once a good bed of coals was established, fewer sticks were added.

Next to him, Jimmy had piled Norway spruce boughs. With his knife he cut the branches into smaller clumps; the green needles left pin prick impressions on his hands. He added several to the coals. They sizzled and spit and gave off a dense white smoke, which rose like a column through the still air. Once above the treetops, it drifted north over the logging road toward the valley beyond.

Jimmy performed the smoke ceremony as best he could. With his eyes clenched shut, he pulled the smoke toward himself guiding it first around his body then over his face and head. He did this several times. Waited for the smoke to clear. Then looked for the wolf. It was not there.

He tried to think of what words to say but none came. He waited. He wished that Hawk had given him some words. He tried the smoke again and coughed. Still no wolf. Finally he decided to be more patient. He would sit there all day if that's what it took. After all, Hawk had said to do this until dark.

He fed the fire and put on more pine boughs. The strong perfume of the smoke made him dizzy. He closed his eyes and listened. The fire fluttered like bird wings. A titmouse called from the laurel. Down the valley near Two Mile Creek a pileated woodpecker knocked on a dead tree dry as a post sounding very much like an Indian drum. High overhead a raven's raspy voice complained to anyone who would listen. Jimmy opened his eyes and watched. The snowy woods seemed to have moved closer. Details he hadn't noticed before captured his attention. Along the length of a snow covered branch that leaned at an angle on a fallen log were tiny mouse tracks side by side like a row of equal signs. The creamy underside of a halfmoon fungus attached to a tree trunk had been carved by some insect larva, worm or beetle. The subtle lines meandered around the surface like trails on a map. Below the fungus the trails continued etched into the bleached trunk, another story that had played itself out long ago leaving only fossil like evidence, petroglyphs from a disappeared tribe.

The steep side of an exposed rock was covered with a blanket of lime green moss. At first Jimmy thought of it as fur. Then he saw it as a great forest in miniature, each stem an old growth tree whose ancient seed sprouted millennia ago. The bright sun laid dark tree shadows across the snow like planks.

Jimmy looked south through the smoke toward the creek. Like fog, the smoke added mystery to the setting. He had the sensation that he was a figure in a painting, a great landscape of forest in winter with a tiny human being tending a fire. He was aware that he was actually looking at himself from a distance. He was in a tree peering down; he was an owl watching. The boy below sat with his knees up, his arms around them. Dark brown hair stuck out from his gray wool cap. The boy's face was tanned from being outdoors so much. An intent face, a patient face with dark eyes like those of a hawk. He was still, motionless by the fire with its gray-blue smoke rising in a column through leafless branches into the great blue dome of the sky.

The morning light shifted, noon passed, the sun drifted like a cold china plate across the sky. Jimmy stoked the fire, added more wood, more pine boughs. He pulled the smoke in. In his mind he began to visualize the wolf. The thick black fur, the full tail, erect ears, the long muzzle, the dark leather of the nose, the intense yellow eyes around which his black hairs parted like water around rock. In his imagination, Jimmy could see Romeo loping along the creek, hear his panting; he could see what the wolf saw, smell what it smelled lingering in the air. It ran with its head close to the ground. Intermittently, it would stop and survey the woods, listen. Then move on.

The sun slipped down into the western mountains. The fire was low. Jimmy put the last of the wood on the coals. When it flared up, he covered the flames with pine boughs. He began to speak. At first in his head, then out loud. "Wolf," he said. Then "Wolf" again. Then over and over as if it were a chant. "I mean you no harm, wolf. Hawk says we are brothers. We should meet. Tell each other stories. Exchange voices. Listen to the woods together. Wolf. Wolf." His voice trailed off to a whisper as he watched the smoky fire.

Jimmy lifted his head higher and stared through the white smoke. Looking back at him was the black wolf. It was fifty yards away standing sideways by a snow-covered boulder. The wolf's head was turned toward Jimmy. Its breath was smoke drifting in gray puffs toward the laurel. Its tail was down. The wolf made no sound, showed no menacing behavior. It just watched Jimmy. Jimmy watched the wolf. He remained still as stone as he had trained himself to do when watching any wild thing, but inside, his heart thudded like a drum beat. He was sure the wolf could hear it. Fear was not pumping blood; joy was. Gradually Jimmy calmed himself, accepted the moment and stayed there allowing the rest of the world to disappear. Yesterday fell away; tomorrow was a vapor burning off. There was only now, the center of the universe, the wolf and Jimmy.

After a few moments, the wolf sat and then, after some time, lay down in the snow with its dark head erect watching. Jimmy did not move for a long time. The fire died down; the smoke became a thin gray line. Finally Jimmy spoke to the wolf. His voice was low and calm. He told the wolf about the tracks he'd found, about his journal and about the things Hawk had taught him. The wolf listened.

Light faded in the woods and went out. Jimmy could hardly see the wolf. It was a dark shadow in the snow. After a long silence, he could see the shadow move off to the south in the direction of the creek. It slipped through the trees like an apparition, silent as a ghost.

As he made his way through the dark to the logging road, Jimmy promised Romeo that he would keep their meeting a secret, except he'd have to tell Hawk.

That night Hawk found Jimmy in the barn carving a stout hiking stick. He asked, "Whatcha got goin' there?"

Jimmy looked up, his face bright with excitement. "I'm carving a wolf's head, but it's not easy."

"You using applewood?"

"Yes."

"Good," said Hawk. "Did you spend some time with that stick to make sure it wants to be a wolf?"

Sometimes it was hard for Jimmy to know when Hawk was just joking with him, but he played along. "I certainly did," he said.

"Then all you gotta do," Hawk explained as he ran his hand along the gray braid of his hair, "is cut away the part that's not wolf and there you are!"

Jimmy smiled. "What I need to do is sharpen this knife. I want to carve the head as if the wolf is howling. That would be best. I think that is what the stick wants."

Hawk gave a broad grin and sat on an overturned milk bucket. In the yellow gleam of the kerosene lantern, both faces appeared like twin moons against the dark cave of the barn.

"I saw him today," Jimmy whispered. He told his old friend every detail of his day up at Two Mile: the smoke ceremony, the signs of life all around him, the appearance of the black shadow that wasn't a shadow, the intense yellow eyes whose gaze he could not turn away from.

Finally Hawk said, "I knew it would be as you have told it. It is a good thing."

5

wj 3 February

The wolf is a predator at the top of the food chain. He feeds on prey animals many times his size. Hunting in packs out west or in Canada, the wolf is able to tackle full-grown buffalo or elk. More often than not they will seek out calves or old or wounded adults. The weaker the animal, the easier the hunt, less risk of injury. By taking the easier quarry, the wolf strengthens the herd. Healthy animals have formidable defenses, horns and hooves that can kill a wolf.

The wolf is also responsible for limiting the size of a herd. This is good for the environment in which they live. Overgrazing is reduced, and there is more food for the healthy animals. The balance of nature is maintained. Take the whitetail deer in our area. Because they have no predator to keep their numbers in check, their population has exploded. They cause accidents, they destroy crops, they strip the forest of much of the vegetation within their reach. More chance of starvation.

A wolf pack will chase a herd for miles testing the endurance of each individual. Once an animal is selected, their attack is relentless and will go on for hours or days, if necessary. Hawk says that a wolf is fed by his feet, which means he has the ability to run long distances in pursuit of prey. Of course, there are no buffalo here for wolves to hunt. There are elk over near St. Marys, but there are none in our valley. We do have whitetail deer and plenty of them. Before Romeo showed up, the only enemies deer had were man, some coyotes, a few wild dogs and a tough winter.

Romeo doesn't have the advantage of a pack. He is a lone wolf as far as I can tell. However, I am certain he is a good hunter. The tracks I found indicated that he was on the trail of a small band of deer. I am confident that he will have plenty to eat.

A wolf provides food for other critters as well. After he has eaten, crows, ravens and turkey buzzards visit the carcass. Smaller animals like bobcats benefit from the leftovers. Coyotes may feed as well, but at great risk. Wolves view them as competitors and will kill them or chase them out of the area.

The wolf is very protective of its territory. The boundary is clearly marked with urine and is patrolled regularly by the wolf. Wolves treat wild dogs the same as coyotes. I have seen these dogs in the woods before. They are very ragged looking. Often I think they kill just for the heck of it, not always for food. The wolf will not do this. Having been domesticated at one time, the wild is gone out of these dogs and they have no respect for it. I would much rather meet a wolf in the wild than one of those mangy curs. I have seen no sign of dogs in the Two Mile area since I found Romeo's tracks.

Much of what I know about wolves comes from talks with Hawk and from my reading about them for several years. Recently, I have been keeping track of the wolf reintroduction program in Yellowstone Park through their web site www.wolf.gov. Dad says we might go there someday to see them first hand. That would be so incredible! The most recent books I've read are *Living with the Pack* by Harriot Mott (She's a biologist in Alaska.), and *Wolf Pup* by Robert Ross who raised a young wolf as a pet. Mr. Ross lives in Montana near Glacier National Park. Both books are filled with great stories and interesting facts about wolf behavior. There is also a guy named Mech who has written a few books about his wolf studies on Isle Royale and in Denali, but our library doesn't have them yet.

I think what I am discovering in keeping this journal is what I'd like to do after high school. Right now I can't imagine anything more exciting than being a field biologist studying wolves in the wild. Yes, I think I'll do that. Mom said she heard on the radio that there is some talk about bringing wolves back to the Adirondack Mountains up in northern New York State. She says that a lot of people are upset about it. I told her that if they knew what I knew, they wouldn't be afraid. Maybe I'll end up helping bring wolves back to Pennsylvania! That would be something.

6

Mr. Fletcher asked Jimmy if he would stay after class for a few minutes so that they could discuss his journal. After the other students left, he sat in a chair next to Jimmy's desk. He adjusted his black and blue plaid tie and rolled up the sleeves of his blue shirt.

"Jimmy," he began, his voice a little deeper than normal, "I've been teaching over twenty years now in this school, and I've never read a journal as good as yours."

"Thank you, Mr. Fletcher," Jimmy said.

"Is this cover real leather?" His hand moved over the brown cover.

"I tanned it myself. Hawk and my dad taught me. The hide came from the first deer I got two years ago."

"You shot a deer?" Fletcher said.

"Oh, not with a gun. My father doesn't like guns. Says they don't give animals a chance. I used a bow. I made that, too, and the arrows. Hawk says it's a way of showing respect. The hunter has to be as wary as the deer when using a bow. Anyway, my father showed me how to cut the hide twice as long as the cover so it could fold back into two inside pockets. After I sewed the edges, he put a cedar shake in each one to make the covers stiff. I sewed an extra piece along the spine to make it stronger. When my father finishes a piece of furniture, he signs his name with a hot pen. That's what I used for the wolf on the cover and my initials on the back." Jimmy stopped talking.

Mr. Fletcher looked at the vocabulary words printed on the green chalkboard and then back at Jimmy. "You certainly did a fine job. How is it that you know so much about wolves?"

Jimmy looked at him puzzled. "Didn't you read my last entry? In it I gave my sources like you asked us to do: the internet, the books and Hawk, my friend. I've been interested in wolves for a long time."

"Yes, I read that. But you seem to know so much. And what about these tracks you found? You really think there's a wolf out there?"

"Oh, no, Mr. Fletcher! You said to 'exercise' our imaginations. That's all I'm doing. Making it up. It's just pretend, that's all. I really enjoy doing that. Is that wrong? Did you mean something else?"

"No, that's what I meant. It's just that you make it seem so real. You are an excellent writer. You have a good vocabulary, Jimmy, and I couldn't find any spelling errors which is something all the other journals certainly have."

"My father always tells me," Jimmy said, "it's not good to make mistakes."

"I thought we might get around to your father, Jimmy." Mr. Fletcher ran his fingers through his brown hair and adjusted his tie again. "From the very specific details and the quality of writing, I suspect that your father has been helping you write these entries. Is that the case, Jimmy?"

Jimmy suddenly felt pale and sick. He'd never been accused of anything before. He looked across the room full of empty desks and out the window where a group of kids were throwing snowballs at one another. Beyond was the woods where he wished he were right now.

His voice cracked as he spoke. "Pa can't hardly read nor write, Mr. Fletcher, except for his name. Ma can do a little better, but she gets words confused sometimes. I'm the first in the family to make it to high school. But they ain't dumb, I mean aren't dumb. They both know the woods and farming. Pa can build a good house even if he can't write a sentence. And Ma, she can cure us kids of ailments by using plants she finds out in the field and back up in the mountains. She can cook anything farm raised or wild. Leek soup. Rattlesnake stew. There's a lot who can read who can't do that. My sisters are still learning, but I'm the only one in the family who can read and write. The journal is my own writing, Mr. Fletcher."

"I'm sorry, Jimmy. This is my fault. I'm just not used to seeing such quality writing from a ninth grade student. You weren't in my class last semester so this is the first thing of yours I've read. Your teacher must have been very good."

"She was, but I read a lot, too," Jimmy said. "When I read, I run into new words and different ways of putting them together. Besides, I like to write. It helps me think, helps me figure things out, helps me to remember."

Mr. Fletcher said, "Well, Jimmy, I hope you'll accept my apology. I'm already looking forward to your next entry. By the way, I really enjoy all those drawings in the margins. You have many talents."

Jimmy's chair scraped the floor as he stood to leave. He was almost out of the classroom door when Mr. Fletcher said, "Jimmy, I hope you get a chance to see Romeo."

Jimmy rushed down the hall to his locker. Even though he was very late for social studies, he stood by his open locker door feeling panic. The lie, he knew, was that he had said the entries were made up. In fact, that was not the case. Everything he wrote was true. The only way to protect Romeo from being found out was by keeping that lie alive. Mr. Fletcher's last words echoed in Jimmy's head. It's possible, he thought, that Mr. Fletcher already knows.

7

When I saw Romeo in the woods, I knew I had nothing to fear. He was standing some distance from me. Although, at first, his face was expressionless, his tail was in a lowered position. Tail position is one way a wolf communicates. A raised tail is a show of dominance or maybe agitation or an indication that he is ready to hunt. A lowered tail could mean subservience (I looked that word up), which means he is willing to accept another wolf as leader or alpha male or female. I think in the case of our meeting, it simply meant that he was not afraid of me, did not feel threatened in any way.

This tail sign is also true of many other animals. The tail of the deer is lowered when they are feeling secure. The white flag goes up if they are in danger. Squirrels flash their tails in rapid motion when they give an alarm call to warn of an intruder who could be a threat. Of course, you already know how a skunk expresses his displeasure. If his tail goes up, look out!

Wolves have many ways to communicate. They use other forms of body language like head and ear position, the baring of teeth as well as cowering or standing erect. All of these send signals to other wolves and other animals like me.

From what I've been able to read, wolves have many vocalizations (another thesaurus word). Some say they howl to assemble for a hunt, but I wonder if it isn't more to sing for the joy of it. Some accounts indicate that wolves are just trying to locate each other. I'll bet that it's a way the pack has of bonding with one another. They also growl fiercely to show anger especially if challenged when feeding. They bark and yip like any dog all of which are descendants of the wolf. I haven't been able to find any scientific explanation for those noises, but I think they are just part of the way wolves talk, to get attention, show pain or excitement or hunger. Romeo made no sounds when I saw him. In fact, he made no noise when he approached or when he left. It was as if he were a ghost wolf.

Wolves are very secretive animals. They stay as far away from humans as they can get. Why this wolf would show himself to me is a great mystery. Hawk says some mysteries are not meant to be solved, just accepted. So I have accepted this one.

Romeo is a magnificent animal whose eyes speak volumes. They are forceful in their focus almost as if he were trying to read my mind. There must have been some telepathy going on. Although I did not speak aloud, my mind was crowded with thoughts, which I tried to arrange into words. As each formed into a clear idea, Romeo seemed to react with subtle changes in his facial expressions the way a dog will respond when he is struggling to understand what you are saying to him. Of course, it's a silly notion that humans can communicate with animals, but the feelings I had during that encounter were more intense than I had ever experienced. What I sensed was the true, wild heart of the mountain, seeing the woods as if for the first time from his point of view.

My vision was sharper so that individual hairs from Romeo's long, black body were clear, distinct. I could separate the stream of woven odors that flowed toward me into isolated strands so that each breath unlocked the subtle secrets that lingered there. Sounds came to me from great distances transforming what I had taken for silence into a chorus of creaks, scrapes, wing beats, hooves muffled by snow, rodent squeaks, and, what seemed to be a gnawing sound coming from under the snow. I became more aware than ever before of the texture of things: rough trunk bark, smooth branch skin, snow crystals powdering the vertical face of a boulder, the dull green sheen of laurel leaves, the stiff, dry fronds of tiny groundpine whose faint heat has softened the snow which surrounds it.

I didn't have a vision the way Hawk describes his elders had when they would disappear into the forest for long periods of time looking for enlightenment. All of this is just my own imagination gone berserk. I don't mind telling you, though, that I really enjoy these make believe adventures. Hawk says that because a considerable part of living our lives happens in our heads, it's important to pay attention to those dreams and daydreams, otherwise, we risk leaving blank so much that makes life interesting.

8

The farmhouse receded from view as the faded red farm truck, an old flatbed Ford with no muffler, rattled and bumped down the dirt road over the plank bridge that spanned Lillibridge Creek and onto the macadam road that led into town. Snow banks were piled high along the berm. It hadn't snowed in a week, and the white mounds were a dusty brown. Further out in the fields where the creek meandered like a dark snake, Jimmy could see trails where deer had crossed having come down out of the woods to forage for twigs along the bank. He took the whole winter scene in in a glance then looked back at the road. He was trying hard to concentrate on his driving.

"This has been a tough winter for deer," Jimmy said raising his voice to be heard over the broken exhaust pipe.

His father said, "That bunch I saw last night was mighty thin. The hides of 'em looked like they was just stretched over bones. You could count ribs sure enough."

The two were silent for a while before his father said, "So in this journal of yours, you writin' all about the wolf you found?"

"Yes, Pa, and drawing pictures."

"Does Fletcher believe a word of it?"

"He told us to use our imaginations so I told him that that is what

I'm doing. I feel badly about fibbing to him about those entries, but I don't want anyone to know about Romeo. You know how some people are around here. Besides the journal sounds all made up. You didn't even believe me at first."

"At first," his father said turning to look at him, "I thought maybe you just had a vision like the ones Hawk's always talking about. I never known a man that sees so much that isn't there. But I got me a bad feelin' about your wolf. There's a lot that hunt these woods, and, as soon as word gets out, they'll be after 'im. And you'll be in for a big bad time, a real heartache."

"But, Pa, aren't wolves protected?"

'Maybe out west, but here no one's going to pay any mind to a law like that. There's guys right here in town who make it their business to know where that ranger fella is every day. Once they've located him, they just go hunt in another part of the county. Woolman's got too big a territory to cover. He did have an assistant a few years ago, Cole I think his name was, but come April of that year, Woolman caught 'im with three bucks hanging in his barn.

"Hey, try to stay in your own lane there, son. The other one belongs to cars comin' the other way."

Jimmy turned the wheel slightly. He felt as though he was getting better at this every time his father let him drive to school, which was whenever he needed to go into town for supplies at the lumberyard.

"That's much better," his father continued. "Now these guys in town are good trackers like yourself. Your wolf can't hide forever unless Romeo is smarter than I think he is. And another thing, whenever farmers hereabout lose some livestock, they'll blame dogs at first, then your wolf. You got to prepare yourself for them having a different opinion when it comes to wolves. I happen to be only part farmer. Building's our livelihood. Farming just helps out. So Romeo don't worry me much. Those who depend on their farms will be mighty concerned."

Jimmy gradually clenched the steering wheel so that his knuckles whitened. His face was serious. He gave a sigh and said, "I know you're right. Even if Romeo doesn't take any cattle or sheep, they'll blame him if they know he's out there. That's why I want this to be a secret. I felt sick last week when Mr. Fletcher asked me if you were helping me write my journal entries."

"That's a good one!" his father laughed.

"I got the feeling he knew it wasn't made up. Maybe I better stop writing about Romeo and just stick to what I find out from books."

His father put his hand on Jimmy's shoulder. "If you do that, he'll get suspicious right off. Now I don't hold with lying unless it's for a mighty good cause. I think you got one right here. So your wolf's best chance is for you to keep writing. By the way, how are you and that young lady getting along?" Jimmy nearly swerved off the road. "Whoa, son."

"I haven't even talked to her yet," Jimmy said with a sigh, which was punctuated by the thunder of the busted exhaust system.

"But you been thinkin' about her, am I right?" his father raised his voice.

Jimmy grinned and nodded yes.

"Well, that's the first step. I thought about yer ma nearly a year before I got up the nerve to ask her out."

"What did she say?"

"As I remember it, she said no. Then I told her the next day that she was probably making a very big mistake and that I was willing to overlook the error and give her a second chance. She had a beautiful smile. She said, 'Thank you for being so thoughtful, but the answer is still no.' You see, Jimmy, the problem was that she was a town girl like your Sherry and, like you, I was raised on the farm. Also, I wasn't in school. She wasn't either. I had to work the farm and she took care of her family's hardware store. I didn't have new clothes and probably smelled like the barn, but I sensed in her second 'no' a slight weakening. It took a week, but by the fifth chance she said yes and I coulda jumped right over Old Baldy. So you keep on trying, son. Ya never know."

Jimmy felt strange thinking of his parents as kids in love, but he liked the story because maybe it would become his story if he ever got up the nerve to say something to Sherry. He worked the clutch down-shifting through the gears, pulled up to the stop sign on Mill Street, turned right, drove to the school and slowed to a stop by the front entrance. The truck jerked and stalled. Jimmy smiled sheepishly at his father and slid out of the truck. His father slid over and said, "Say hi to Sherry for me!" and roared off. Jimmy could hear the truck backfire with each shift of the gears as it moved down Arnold Avenue.

He was late. Fletcher's first period English had already begun. He entered as quietly as he could, handed Fletcher his pass and took his seat.

"As I was saying," Fletcher continued as he paced up and down rows making that eye contact that kept everyone listening, "writing is seeing, using very specific detail. You can't assume that your audience can see everything you see in your head. You have to spell it out. The more specific details you include, the more three dimensional your writing will be.

"As beginning writers some of us use general words rather than specific ones. 'It was a beautiful day' someone wrote in one of their entries. How much richer that entry would have been if the writer had created on paper exactly what made that day beautiful. Beautiful is an empty canvas. Was the sky clear blue with some cumulus clouds floating above the mountains like the sails of distant ships? Were the fields strewn with wildflowers: Queen Anne's Lace, buttercups, tiger lilies, blood red wild rose? Were the leaves of maples and oaks shuddering in the wind like a whisper? Was the scent of pine in the air? Were jays calling? Was the wood thrush singing its flute like song in the deep woods? Get the picture?"

He loosened his tie, removed a pen from his shirt pocket and wrote a sentence in the air with it. When he got to the period, he said, "And that's the whole point. Getting the picture. Creating a detailed image that your reader can see in their head so that they know exactly what you mean by 'a beautiful day'."

"But, Mr. Fletcher," Sherry said, "How are we supposed to know all those things?"

Jimmy watched her knowing that she could not look back while Fletcher was talking to her.

Fletcher said, "Most of what I just told you, you already know. The names of flowers, birds and trees you can look up in a field guide. They're in the library along with a lot of other good stuff. I believe it is our responsibility as writers to be curious enough about the world around us to want to know the names of things. If a boy sends you flowers," he waited for the giggling to die down, "they aren't just flowers. They have a name!"

"Dandelions!" Big Charlie blurted out.

The class erupted except for Jimmy. Sherry turned and covered her face. Jimmy stared at his desk so that no one would guess what he was thinking.

Fletcher said, "Charles, have you received flowers lately?"

"Anyone sends me flowers, I'll punch 'em in the head!" he said making a fist.

"I think, Charles, if you keep cracking jokes in here, someone will send you flowers. The whole football team will hear about it and they'll start calling you Daisy or Petunia. Get the picture, Charles?"

Several boys in the back called out Big Charlie's new nicknames.

"I got it, Mr. Fletcher," Big Charlie whispered.

Jimmy certainly didn't want anyone to get the picture he had in his head. It was a movie that he played over and over in his imagination. Unlike his wolf journal, it wasn't true. But the details were so vivid that it seemed to be. He certainly wished it were so. He had been sitting near Sherry since seventh grade both having last names that began with 'w'. In eighth grade when they were asked to write poems, he called his *Falling in Love in Alphabetical Order*. As his feelings for Sherry grew, so did the intensity of his daydreams.

In his imagination Sherry was walking down the hall toward his locker from which he had just removed his afternoon books and notebooks. He stood there with his hand on the open door watching her walk. Her light brown hair was pulled back in a ponytail, which swung from side to side as she approached. She reminded him so much of the painting *Girl with Book* which hung in the school lobby. She was holding an open book, but her gaze did not focus on it. Jimmy was sure the girl in the painting was daydreaming like he so often did. Sherry could have been the model for that painting. Her sea green eyes looked straight at him. She had an oval, doll's face with high cheekbones, a slender nose and skin as pale and soft as an October moon. Sherry smiled and parted her lips as if she were about to speak. She wore a white, knit sweater and a short, black skirt. The curves of her body moved gracefully along the deserted hall. Every time Jimmy had this dream the halls were empty. There was only the two of them.

He closed the locker door slowly without taking his eyes off her. She said, "Hello, Jimmy." Her arms encircled his neck, and she pressed her lips to his. He pulled her close and felt dizzy from the subtle smell of her perfume, a whole field of wildflowers, a mixture of Queen Ann's Lace, buttercups, tiger lilies and wild roses.

In his dream, hand in hand, they'd walk to the bench by Lillibridge Creek where it flowed near the school. Cumulus clouds floated in a blue sky. Wind vibrated the leaves of the old maple where he one day hoped to carve their initials. The stream talked quietly as it ran over rocks and spilled silvery light on the far bank. Jimmy showed Sherry his journal. He told her everything. About finding the tracks, about the smoke ceremony, about seeing Romeo. He showed her the drawings, pencil sketches of birds, deer, all manner of tracks, trees, rocks and, of course, the wolf.

He knew in his dream that he could trust Sherry with his secret, and that she would love him even more because he had shared his most prized experience with her. He would tell her, in his dream, about becoming a wolf biologist tracking packs in the snowcapped mountains of Wyoming, the long valleys of Montana or along the Salmon River in Idaho where he read there were wild wolves. Or maybe even up in New York State, in the Adirondacks. He was certain that by the time he was ready to go out on his own, wolves would be back in that mountain range.

Sherry, too, would reveal her life dreams although because he had not even spoken to her yet, he could not imagine what those dreams would be. But they were always compatible with his, which allowed this daydream of his to be just the first chapter of the long novel of their life together.

"Getting the picture from your head into the reader's head is the whole trick of writing well," Fletcher said. "Some of you are already using words that are very specific to your subject. Shank, a part of a hook, and stonefly from flyfishing; megabyte and font from computers; scat and territory from wolf tracking; trajectory and shaft from archery. Some of you, too, really let your passion show in your writing. You have good imaginations. Next week, like I promised, I'll be asking a few of you to select an entry to read aloud."

The bell rang. Class ended. Jimmy gathered his books together and moved to the door with the others. Someone brushed his arm. He turned. It was Sherry, smiling, her green eyes locked on his. "Hello, Jimmy," she said.

His heart clenched. He could not draw breath in order to respond. He could feel a flush of red come to his face. Jimmy forced out a weak "Hilo", a panicked hybrid of hi and hello. Quickly he moved into the hall where the stream of kids whisked him along as he muttered to himself, "How could I say that? It's not even a word. She must think I'm an idiot. What a complete jerk. Not cool, not cool." In the main lobby he passed *Girl with Book* and silently said to her, "I'm so sorry."

9

*H*awk says that the circle is a sacred symbol to most American Indian tribes. In a kind of spiritual way it represents the power of life. He said that many of the rituals of his people were done in a circle around a fire ring or a medicine wheel. There was an ancient medicine wheel not far from here on a peak to the south near Emporium or St. Marys. Hawk said when he was a boy, he had visited it many times to pray. It had a large central cairn, an igloo shaped pile of rocks, with six smaller cairns arranged in a circle twenty feet from the center. The outer cairns were connected with a row of rocks creating a great circle. The rim was joined to the central cairn by many rock spokes. Hawk remembered that his family hiked there several times a year and had great dances with all night fires. He said that the elders would offer prayers. Then the singing began and continued late into the night. He said what fascinated him were the bright sparks from the fire and the sky full of stars. The stars were so bright that often he couldn't tell which was which. But vandals destroyed that wheel. It was erased. The only thing that remained were the impressions in the ground where the rocks had been. Soon that too was gone.

When he was in his thirties, he heard of another medicine wheel that was still in tact and still used by western tribes. He rode a train alone from Buffalo, New York to Buffalo, Wyoming in the foothills of the Big Horn Mountains. He hiked many days to Medicine Mountain. The top of the mountain, about nine thousand feet, was the top of the world covered with exposed gray rock from which you could see for miles. Ancient trails used by tribes for centuries converged from the four directions near an immense medicine wheel. There was a fence around it, but because he was Susquehannock, he was allowed in to perform his ceremonies, say his prayers and stay all night if he wished. He stayed four nights.

One of the things Hawk told me about that trip was that it brought back the memory of offerings he had made at the 'disappeared' wheel of his youth. Once he left deer horns tied together with leather thongs. Another time he had left a necklace he had made of stones. He also remembered leaving a leather bag, a medicine bag, containing roots, bones and a cateye marble that he valued.

Hanging from the fence at the Wyoming Medicine Wheel were hundreds of offerings left by former visitors. There were exquisite bead sacks, leather necklaces, and feather bouquets sewed to bone or antlers. There were bandannas and ribbons of blue, red, green and yellow all fluttering in the wind that 'lived on the mountain' like a flock of colorful birds. Someone had left a pair of child's moccasins with a picture of the little girl who had gone to live in the other world. Another had left a circle of leather upon which was a likeness of a brave on a painted horse hunting a buffalo. The image was woven from porcupine quills. An old woman from Pine Ridge Reservation arrived while Hawk was still there. She left a colorful sash she had made which contained many symbols that told the history of her family. She also taught Hawk the power of 'thought prayer' which flows directly from the heart. She said it was how her animal brothers have communicated since the beginning.

Hawk had forgotten to bring an offering to leave at the Medicine Wheel. So to show respect for this spiritual place at the top of the world, he tied the hawk feathers he was wearing in his hair to the outer fence. The feathers had been given to him at his birth along with his name.

The whole point, Hawk said to me, was to show respect and give thanks. "Great power comes to those who give thanks. Sometimes that power comes in the form of a vision that enlightens, brings understanding of how the world is or will be. Sometimes it comes in the form of a gift like seeing a wolf."

So last Saturday I hiked up to the head of Two Mile Creek arriving before daybreak. I was determined to try the smoke ceremony again and to leave an offering. This time I built the fire in a circle and tied a hide medicine bag I had made to a pine bough nearby. It contained some old coins, some dried corn kernels, a ring of winter grass I had collected from the bank of Lillibridge Creek and a bit of pine bark from the tree outside my bedroom window. I would have left the walking stick, but I haven't finished carving it yet. The wolf head is finished, but I want to include much more: a grip of vines, a fire circle, tracks, a few deer, the stream, the medicine bag. Maybe I forgot to mention the wolf stick before. I started carving it several weeks ago. When I finish it in the spring, I'll leave it at the rendezvous site (near Two Mile) as a tribute, an offering.

I walked in a circle starting left as Hawk had instructed. The wolf moves in a circle scent marking his territory. I was emulating (see thesaurus again) the wolf. I couldn't think of any words to say so I just said aloud some secrets I keep as if I was just talking to Romeo. Then I sat still adding pine boughs to the fire. I sat all morning in the silent snow. Sometimes I could hear chickadees, blue jays and squirrels. For the most part, though, quiet inhabited the woods.

The contrast between the heat, smoke and crackle of the fire and the icy silence of the woods was wonderful. It was as if the fire were the burning heart of the woods. I felt privileged to be there. The energy was very strong, and I knew that Romeo would come. In my imagination I could see him loping along Two Mile Creek stepping over rocks, gracefully leaping over windfalls, raising his head occasionally to read the wind. His black fur, a shadow against the snow. He stopped at a bend in the creek where slow water whispered. His ears erect, alert;

those yellow eyes reading the trail. He scent marked the base of a shagbark hickory and continued moving left in a great circle.

I think Hawk was right about the power of the circle. I could feel Romeo's approach before I saw him. He was much closer this time, not more than twenty-five yards away. He stood for a while looking toward the laurel patch. Then he turned, faced me and lay down with his head erect as if he were watching the smoke rise.

The two of us watched each other for some time. When I spoke to him, he cocked his head sideways as if puzzled. Even though I knew he could not understand me, I told him that it was so amazing that he was here in these mountains. I told him what my father had said about the men in town who knew how to track and might hunt him down. I told him that he must be careful not to show himself in the valley and that if he killed any cattle or sheep, it would be the end of him. I said, too, that he should only howl in the deep woods.

He listened.

I kept my voice soft so as not to alarm him. For a little while he put his head down on his extended forepaws. His whole body was black bear black except where the sun shown along the curve of his great neck and the upper crest of his rounded haunches where the dark fur had a slight purple sheen to it like the way a grackle's feathers will change color in strong light.

Romeo made no reply to my long talk. He certainly didn't understand a word of it. I had hoped he would whine or bark, but he only communicated with his eyes. They seemed to look into me, deep into the center of what I thought and felt. Maybe he understood more than I gave him credit for. Maybe he knew that he was a misfit in this place that was once his home.

Because I dared not move, the fire finally burned itself out; and when the last curl of gray smoke rose to the sky and disappeared, so did Romeo. I didn't even see him go. He just vanished.

Hawk says that often it is difficult to tell the difference between a vision and the real thing. If the vision's power is strong, the details of it are as clear as if it really happened. In fact, he believes the vision experience is as real as are those things we encounter in the physical

world. One happens in the outer world; the other occurs in the inner
world of our mind. As I hiked through the deep snow of the logging
road that sloped toward Lillibridge Creek and home, I wondered which
world Romeo lived in.

10

"Your girlfriend's father stopped by just a little bit ago," said Jimmy's mother nonchalantly as she placed a plate of scrambled eggs, corned beef hash and toast in front of her son. Jimmy's face went taut; his eyes widened in panic. "You were busy down in the barn. How'd you and your dad make out with that cow?"

"Fine! She'll be fine! What did he want?"

"Who?"

"Mr. Woolman!" Jimmy gasped.

She placed a glass of orange juice next to his plate. A slat of sunlight from the kitchen window lay across the oak table. Coffee perked on the old cook stove. "Oh, he just wanted to know when you were going to ask that daughter of his out."

"Ma, don't say that. What did he want? What was he doing out here?"

Jimmy's father came in through the kitchen door and removed his rubber boots.

"Put those awful things outside, Joe," Martha said.

"Good mornin', sweet." Joe tossed the boots out the door where they landed on the porch like a pair of muddy flippers. He closed the door and said, "Wasn't that Woolman's truck I saw headin' out our road? What'd he want so early in the mornin'?"

"Wanted to know when that son of ours was going to ask his sweet daughter out on a date?" said Martha.

"Been wonderin' that same thing myself. How exactly we goin' ta get any grandchildren with this one just spendin' all his free time wandering in circles out in the woods. No women out there, Jimmy." Joe smiled at his exasperated son.

Jimmy lowered his shoulders in defeat and poked at his eggs with his fork.

"Jimmy, we're just teasing," Martha said. "He wanted to know if we had any trouble here with wild dogs. Said Nelson down by Steele Hollow lost some sheep a few days ago and that Old Man Swanson next to him found a dead yearling milker right up behind the barn just yesterday. With no snow recently, he said they left a bunch of tracks. Said it couldn't be coyotes because the tracks were too big."

"How big?" said Jimmy looking a little pale.

"Said they was big dogs, shepherds most likely. He figured there was four of them. They didn't even eat the meat, just killed the critters and left. Isn't that a little strange?"

Joe watched his son's face and then he looked at Martha who stood by the stove fixing his breakfast plate. "Dogs'll do that. Kill for killin' sake. Remember when I shot those three mongrels up by the woodlot last spring. Every one of 'em had collars. They either run off or were dropped off in the woods by someone, abandoned. You can't do that to a domestic animal and expect it to survive or act natural in any way. They don't know how. The wild's been bred out of 'em. A wolf on the other hand would eat his fill and come back later to finish off the carcass. I doubt that this is the work of your wolf, Jimmy."   .

"It can't be! It's too far from his territory. I'll go down and measure the prints. That'll tell for sure."

Martha said, "Here come Lewis and Hawk. I better put on some more eggs. Jimmy, you finish that plate before you run off, you hear. Where are those sisters of yours? It's nearly seven and they haven't stirred yet."

Jimmy hiked the four miles down the plowed road to Nelson's farm. As he walked, there was a clutter of conversations going on in his head. 'This better not be you, Romeo. You live too far away.' 'Wolves are fed by their feet. They'll roam many miles in a single day to find food.' 'Romeo, there are so many deer in your own territory, how could you do this?' 'I wonder if Sherry was with her dad this morning. I could have said something to her. Oh, sure, as if she wanted to hear anything from me.' 'These farms are too far from Romeo's range. Maybe Hawk will help me track the perimeter, his boundary to prove he didn't do it. Next they'll be offering a reward. What then? How will you save yourself now, wolf?' 'I wish I could show you to Sherry, but her warden dad would find out and pow! you'd be gone from here for another hundred years. Ma and Pa are right. I have to talk to you soon, Sherry, or die of miserableness. I wonder if there's such a word. Well, I sure feel it.'

And so it went all the way to the Nelson farm. When he arrived, Mrs. Nelson answered the door. She was a slight woman, seemed even a little sickly to Jimmy. Her face was deeply wrinkled like an eroded stream bank, gray hair all tangled as a bird's nest and her arms and hands were just bone covered by saggy skin with a roadmap of blue veins.

She said that Mr. Nelson, as she referred to her husband, was in town running errands, but Jimmy was welcome to have a look around. "If you see those dirty varmints, blow their goddamn brains out!" she said and slammed the door.

Deep in the recesses of his imagination Jimmy heard a rifle shot and saw Romeo fall.

"Thanks, Mrs. Nelson," he said to the closed door. He headed up to the sheep pens. Tracks were everywhere. The carcasses had been removed, but the snow was still stained with crimson blood. The farmer and the warden had trampled some of the tracks. Enough were in tact, however, for him to study. In his pocket notebook he sketched individual tracks showing heal and toe pads. Then he drew them in a series to illustrate gait pattern and length of stride. Finally, he measured width,

length and depth of several tracks. They were a full inch shorter than
Romeo's, and that was not allowing for snow melt which always makes
a print larger. The tracks were deep, though, even where the 'dirty
varmints' stood still. The dogs probably weighed eighty or ninety pounds.
Romeo was closer to a hundred twenty or thirty pounds. These were
definitely dog tracks. Maybe three dogs, Jimmy thought, all about the
same size. Snagged on the barbed wire fence were clumps of black and
brown fur. German shepherds, Jimmy said to himself.

At Old Man Swanson's farm, Jimmy did the same with the same
results. Swanson followed him up to the kill site cursing with more
colorful language and much more force than Mrs. Nelson. Jimmy let
him rant as if there was anything he could do about it. When he finished measuring and drawing the tracks, he told Swanson who was red
in the face from all his hard talk that these were the same dogs who got
Nelson's sheep. Jimmy left for home leaving Old Man Swanson up by
the barn swearing aloud about his dead cow as if he were addressing an
invisible audience of victims of injustice whose sympathy he hoped to
win.

At dinner Jimmy showed all present his notebook sketches and
measurements, and explained the conclusions he drew from these ob-
vious facts as if he were a lawyer defending Romeo. The jury agreed
that Romeo was innocent. He went on to describe his encounters with
Mrs. Nelson and Swanson paraphrasing their stronger expletives. Martha
said that Mrs. Nelson must be near ninety and that Old Man Swanson
was called that back when she was Jimmy's age.

Lewis made a long face, narrowed his eyes and said, "They're both
just bitter folks because their youngens growed and moved away. They
ain't got no one to leave their farm to. As soon as they kick the bucket,
those kids of theirs will sell off the farms, and houses will go in there.
The least little thing gets them going."

"I wouldn't call having your cow or sheep killed a little thing," Joe
said cutting another slice of meatloaf.

"If you been farming full time like they have, you got to expect
some losses. The trick in farming is not to lose everything. If you can

do that, you've made a success of it," Lewis said scratching the stubble of his gray beard.

"Hawk," Jimmy said, "are you busy tomorrow?"

"What day is it?"

"Sunday."

"It depends," said Hawk.

"I was wondering if you'd like to help me figure out Romeo's territory. I could probably do it, but I sure would like some company."

"Why do you need to know that?" Hawk asked.

"I just wanted to see if he gets near any farms. I think he sleeps up near the Rocks on Saddleback."

"You want to go before or after church?"

"Hawk, you don't even go to church."

"You do."

"Oh, I forgot." Jimmy turned to his mother. "Ma, do I have to?"

"You'll have to ask your father. He's the one around here that has the most experience in missing Sunday services."

Joe smiled at the mild criticism. "I think as long as you're spending the day in the woods, I can't see the difference."

Little Sally spoke up, "Well, isn't anyone going to tell Jimmy what happened today before I burst. Can I tell him? Can I?"

"You let me do it, young lady. You'll just tease him. Grown ups don't do that sort of thing." Martha smiled.

"Tell me what? What'd I miss?"

"While you were out all day making those beautiful sketches, you got a phone call. A certain young lady was wondering if you might call her when you got in. She said she had some questions about the journals you both were writing. I said I'd pass the message on."

"It was Sherry!" exclaimed Maureen wagging a finger at her brother.

"I wanted to tell him," Sally pouted.

Jimmy stood up. "She called here? Why didn't you tell me? She's been waiting all this time?"

In her calmest voice, his mother said, "I doubt she's been sitting by the phone exactly. I told her you wouldn't be back 'til dark and that you'd call after supper."

"I gotta call her now!" Jimmy said.

"Sit and finish your plate. Then you can call."

Jimmy's face went dark and sullen. As he sank back down into his chair, his father said, "Martha, my sweet, remember we were wondering just this morning about these two love birds who haven't said so much as a word to each other yet? I think we should let the boy go if he excuses himself properly."

"May I please, please be excused?" Jimmy pleaded.

"I guess it's okay if your matchmaker father says so," said Martha.

"Go along, son," Joe said.

Jimmy knocked his chair over when he jumped up. He did not stop to pick it up.

11

wj 12 February

My father says that I sometimes live too much in my imagination, that I need to deal with more real facts, real situations. So I thought for this entry I'd retell some stories of actual wolf sightings in Wyoming, which have been posted on the internet at www.wolfsight.net. Each of these recent accounts is from people who have visited the Lamar Valley in Yellowstone where the Druid Peak Pack is often visible.

Doug Brown from California wrote: July 11th was supposed to be my last day in the park. It was the third day I had been standing along the road near an occupied den site. People arrive here by five a. m. and stay 'til nine or so. Then they return around six p. m. and stay 'til dark. There were about twenty of us this morning, a few with spotting scopes, most with binoculars. People were looking in all different directions scanning the distant grassy flats where the Lamar River ran, looking along the steep banks of Soda Butte Creek which flowed close by, and searched the shadows of the tree line almost a thousand yards across a field on the other side of the road. The pack was known to still be using the den up in those woods, but the area was closed to the public. This is as close as we could get. It was very cold, in the 30s. Some people there had seen the wolves before and had stories to tell about different dramatic sightings.

The first rays of sunlight appeared on the flats. The creek water was steaming. Yesterday I had seen three river otters playing along the bank. Already this morning we had spotted about forty buffalo, a lone, honey-colored grizzly way off on a grassy summit, eight pronghorn antelope grazing in the sagebrush, and a golden eagle circling above the rocky face of Druid Peak. Although I could not see them, sandhill cranes screeched from the tall grass and sage out on the flats.

It was just before six when I heard the first howl, long and lonesome, come from the thick stand of lodgepole pines in which the den was hidden. That cry was joined by two more, then three more, then another. Their chorus filled the entire woods. It was as if I were standing in a cathedral listening to a sacred choir. I felt a chill throughout my body like an electric current. I felt, too, that their song was not really lonesome, but more of a statement saying 'We are here, back in the wild!', a kind of wolf joy, if such a thing is possible. The singing only lasted a few minutes but left a lasting impression on me.

Within minutes a large female wolf appeared in the field five hundred yards from us. Her back was dark gray growing lighter toward her belly, which was white. Her muzzle, head and ears were dark, but her chin and legs were almost white. A guy who had seen her before let me look through his scope. "Alpha female, the mother wolf," he said. She was magnificent.

She lay down in the tall sagebrush. I could hardly see her, just her back and, occasionally, her ears. Then a smaller black wolf appeared with two pups, both gray like their mother. Someone identified the black wolf with a number (they are given numbers rather than names), but I don't remember what it was. She said the black wolf was a sub-adult, two years old, who often babysat the pups while the rest of the pack hunted.

What truly amazed me was that there was nothing between those wolves and me except wildflowers and sagebrush. This was no zoo.

This was real wilderness finally restored to a true balance. I thought to myself, America has really done something right this time!

The wolves stayed in view almost twenty minutes. When they disappeared, I returned to my campsite and renewed my reservations there for ten more days.

May Rutledge wrote her account on July 15th: At 6 a. m. we climbed part way up a hill just downstream from the confluence of Soda Butte Creek and the Lamar River. There were already a dozen people on a small flat area with their scopes set up. My husband wasn't along because it was opening day for cutthroat trout on the Yellowstone River. Both kids were with me, though. Julie and Tommy were very cranky about having to be awake so early. They got over that quickly because the wolves had already been spotted. They were across the river on a flat near a cluster of dry gullies. There was one gray adult and four pups. Two were gray; two were black. One of the black pups was huge, almost twice the size of the others. I'm sure he'll become an alpha male with his own pack. He was the only one sitting up, alert. The others were sprawled out near each other trying to sleep.

We had our own scope so we had a good view. Several people told us to look way left, a few thousand yards near a broken tree. Julie spotted them first. Running in a big circle was a huge dark brown grizzly sow trailed by three cubs. The cubs were adorable, just balls of light brown fur no bigger than a footstool. It was comical watching them try to keep up with their mother. They often stood up on their hind legs to look over the sagebrush.

Meanwhile, way to the right, two more wolves showed up. They had been out hunting or were just returning from a kill site. All five wolves greeted them excitedly with wagging tails and full body rubs. The pups kept licking the mouths of the two new adults, a black and a gray. They in turn regurgitated partially digested meat for the pups. Julie was disgusted. Tommy thought it was cool. A biologist who was in the group explained to the kids that the adults would continue to supply food this way until the pups were old enough to hunt and eat raw meat. He also said that the large black wolf was the alpha male and the gray was the alpha female, parents of the pups.

As soon as the food was regurgitated, the real drama began. The biologist said, "Look at the bears!" The sow must have gotten wind of the pups' food because she was running full speed in their direction. The three cubs were strung out behind her. She closed in on the wolves to within five hundred yards when the two alpha wolves went out to confront her. When they were about a hundred yards apart, the sow turned sharply left. At first the cubs did not realize that their mother had changed directions. They were still running straight at the two wolves. The sow must have given some sort of verbal command because all three turned at once and ran to catch up.

Even though the wolves stopped their pursuit, the bears kept running. Their speed was startling. So fast. Once, though, the lead cub tired and stopped. The two behind it crashed into it, and they all spilled over, scrambled to their feet and ran in different directions for a moment. Then they rushed once again to catch up with the sow. A mile up the valley the bears disappeared beyond the tree line. The alpha wolves rejoined the group, which had already finished eating. The pups begged for more, but there was no more to give.

The total time of the wolf/bear encounter was no more than ten or fifteen minutes. The biologist said that it was difficult to tell what the sow would have done if she didn't have the cubs with her. She might have done battle with the wolves. And if so, the outcome could have gone either way. The interactions between bears and wolves were one of the things being studied in the park. Julie asked if the wolves would go back to the den today. The biologist said he thought they were no longer using the den because the pups were big enough to start learning how to hunt. Once the den was abandoned, the pack set up rendezvous sites like this one where some of the six pups would stay with a sitter while the others hunted. That way they wouldn't lose track of each other.

The one disappointment this morning was that we didn't get to hear the wolves howl. I would have loved it if they did. It would have been a sound of the wild that Julie and Tommy would have remembered the rest of their lives. As it is, they'll certainly remember this morning. One other interesting thing was that during this whole chase there were ten antelope and a pair of Sand Hill Cranes close to the action. They just kept feeding. They'd check on who was where every once in a while, but they never left.

We stayed for another hour and a half watching the wolves, but all they did was sleep.

Idaho Bob has seen the wolves many times and posts all his sightings on the website. This short one was for August 1st: I was several miles downstream from Buffalo Ranch, the ranger station where the Yellowstone Institute is located. I had cooked up some breakfast on a rock at a pulloff and was watching a northern harrier hunt. This hawk glided slowly just inches above the sage. His flight was easy to follow with my scope. Each time he'd spot a ground squirrel, he'd stop in mid air pumping his huge wings before he'd drop onto the unsuspecting squirrel.

I was following his glide path around nine o'clock when he stopped suddenly and dropped out of the scope's field of vision. Before I could lower the scope, I realized I was looking at a wolf. A second wolf soon came into view. They were both females: #42 and #103. Beyond them on a low plateau were two pronghorn. I watched as the wolves ran at the antelope. The antelope ran away a short distance then suddenly turned and ran at the wolves. The wolves turned and ran about a hundred yards and lay down. The antelope stopped and stamped their feet. Then the wolves charged them again.

This went back and forth for a good half hour. Eventually the wolves and pronghorn disappeared over a ridge out of sight. I've seen this behavior several times before. Biologists tell me that antelope will charge wolves when they are trying to defend their young. I didn't see any young nearby. Because of the rolling terrain, many sightings are like this one. You only get to see one act of the play. To be there for the climax, the final curtain is truly a rare thing.

I realize, Mr. Fletcher, that this may not count as a real entry because I just copied down what others wrote. But their sightings give me the feeling as if I were right there with them. Can you imagine that? There are many other tales of sightings in the Lamar Valley. I'll save some for a later journal entry. Many are very emotional. One guy wrote that a lady told him that the first time she saw the wolves she had to sit in the car so no one would see her cry. She said that later she realized that what she had seen was a glimpse of a perfect world, a world in balance, a world she desperately wanted to be a part of. He wrote that she quoted somebody who said 'man was the only animal who fouled his own nest.' So she was weeping for two reasons: for the beauty she saw in the wolves, and for those parts of the world just over the horizon that were so out of tune. The man said in his entry that he didn't confess to her the fact that the first time he saw the wolves he had the same reaction.

It must be intense, don't you think, Mr. Fletcher, to see something so magnificent, free and wild? It makes you think of your own role in the great scheme of life. Where does man fit in? Where does he belong in relation to the wild planet he lives on? Is he apart from Nature or a part of Nature? I think seeing a wolf in the wild would help answer those questions.

12

*J*immy dialed the number and listened to the phone ring at the other end of the line. His grip felt wet. Sweaty palms, he thought. Don't be nervous, he whispered. What'll I say? His mind raced. He took several deep breaths. He heard his sisters giggle in the hallway where they had positioned themselves in order to eavesdrop on his conversation. Someone answered the phone just as Jimmy shouted, "You two beat it! Get out of here!"

"Excuse me?" said the man's voice on the line.

"Oh, my," stammered Jimmy. "I'm sorry. I didn't mean you. My sisters were being silly and I . . . uh."

"Is this Jimmy?" the voice asked.

"Yes, sir, it is."

"This is Sherry's father. She's been waiting for you to call. I was just out to your place this morning, Jimmy, to see about those dogs. Any sign of 'em?"

"No, sir, but I did go have a look at the tracks at Nelsons and Swansons. You were right. Three, maybe four dogs, seventy to eighty pounds apiece, shepherds most likely. I found some fur on the barbed wire."

"That's really good," Mr. Woolman said. "I had heard that you were pretty good at this sort of thing. I especially like people who agree with me. I hear, too, that you found yourself a wolf."

Jimmy suddenly felt faint. It was a punch in the stomach that came out of nowhere. He reddened. His face grew hot. "Oh, that," he muttered trying to cover his lie, "that, well, he's just an imaginary wolf, a made up wolf. Mr. Fletcher said we could do that so I just made him up."

"Well, you got yourself one powerful imagination. No wolves in these old mountains, not for a very long time."

"Yes, Mr. Woolman. That's true enough."

"Let me get my daughter for you. She's been asking every ten minutes if you called yet. Just hold on."

Asking every ten minutes, Jimmy repeated to himself. That's a good sign.

Cradling the phone on his shoulder, he rubbed both of his palms on his jeans to dry the sweat. He could hear his heartbeat in his left temple. His breath was gone. Snap out of it, a voice in his head told him. You've come face to face with a wolf. This can't be that hard. Loosen up.

This is harder, another voice said. Maybe she knows what you've been thinking. Lips on lips. That old Indian woman told Hawk that animals could communicate without speaking. You're an animal. Get the picture? Sherry already knows.

"Hello," said a silk voice on the phone.

All of Jimmy's systems shut down. He could no longer hear his heartbeat or breathe in. He felt sweat trickle down his back.

"Hello," the voice said again.

"Uh, hello. Sherry?" he wheezed out.

"Jimmy? You sound out of breath," Sherry said, her voice a bird song in Jimmy's ear.

"Oh, yes, that, well, I've been working out, running around and all, you know, to keep in shape."

"But you work on the farm," Sherry said puzzled. "You seem to be in pretty good shape to me."

Sweat broke out in small beads on Jimmy's forehead. You've got to relax, he told himself. "Well, thank you. I try. My mom said you called which is why I called you to let you know I got the message you . . ." Jimmy paused. "I'm saying too much, aren't I?"

"Oh, no, not at all. I just wanted to talk to you, ya know, about our journals. When you read your entry in class yesterday, I was really moved by it, I guess. That beautiful Indian story about Shadow and the *Going Away Tale*. I could tell from what you wrote how sensitive you are. I could never write an entry like that."

Jimmy was trying to memorize every note of Sherry's voice so that he could replay them later. "Oh, sure you could," he said feeling calmed by her compliments.

"I have to read one of my entries on Monday and I'm like scared to death because I don't have any entries like yours."

"Well, you wouldn't because you're you and I'm me. We're writing about different things." Jimmy's mother walked through the kitchen and gave him a sly smile. He reddened and continued in more of a whisper, "It's hard to get any privacy around here."

"I know what you mean," Sherry whispered back.

"So what are you writing about?" Jimmy asked.

"Fly fishing," she said in a voice soft as a line curling out over a sunlit stream.

"Fly fishing!? I thought Ricky or Aaron or Big Charlie was doing that?"

"No. It's me. I've been fishing since I was five. Started fly fishing when I was eight. Besides, those guys are all doing school sports. Poor Mr. Fletcher has to read all those entries. He's really not much of a sports guy. I asked him once what he liked to do when he's not teaching and he said 'Think'. What kind of answer is that?"

"He's a little strange, for sure, but I've noticed that all the English teachers we've had are a little wacky. Don't you think so?"

Sherry sighed, "Oh yes. Old Miss Lattimore, last year, dressed every day as if it was still 1969. Remember her tiedyed tee shirts, those stone beads and the fresh flower in her hair?"

Jimmy laughed. He was feeling more comfortable. He sensed his muscles unknotting. He said, "She'd always be humming *Tambourine*

Man or *I Ain't Gonna Work on Maggie's Farm No More.* All I had to do to get an *A* was to quote a few lines from a Dylan song." Sherry laughed. This was a good sign, Jimmy thought. "That's exciting, though, that you're writing about fly fishing. Your journal must be wonderful."

"It's not, really. All I've been writing is facts like rod weight, line size, reel selection. And about insects and how to imitate them, imitate the different stages: nymph, emerger, adult. The Stonefly Nymph is one of my favorites. And the Dark Cahill."

"That sounds good to me. I'd love to learn all that stuff. What's not to like?"

"Well, when I write it down, it seems so flat, so boring. I guess what I'm learning is that I don't have much of an imagination. What am I supposed to do, Jimmy, pretend I'm a bug?"

Jimmy loved it when she said his name. It sounded as though she needed him, was depending on him. It felt good.

Jimmy said, "Have you written about actual fishing?"

"I wrote a really long entry on techniques of casting, the roll cast, the side cast, how to cast in bad weather. And I wrote another entry on matching the hatch, how to read a stream. I always take my tying junk with me so I can create a fly while I'm right there looking at what the trout are feeding on. Both of those entries were sorta good, but still just facts like the one I wrote on tying flies that explains how to use bobbins, what a whip finisher and a hair stacker are and how to hold hackle pliers. I mean like who wants to read about a nail knot, a surgeon's knot or the perfection loop?"

"I would," said Jimmy. "You could pretend that you're fishing on a famous river out west. Do you know any?"

"My dad is always talking about going to Oregon and fishing the Deschutes and Mckenzie Rivers. They're in the Cascade Mountains somewhere. But I don't know what they look like."

"You could make that part up, or, better yet, look it up on the net. Just type in the river name and fly fishing and pictures will show up all over the place. Maybe you could write about the first time you went fly fishing. Have you done that yet?"

"No, but I remember it clearly. I still have a pinhole scar on the back of my neck where I snagged myself. I'll show it to you on Monday." Jimmy pictured Sherry sweeping her hair away from her neck so he could see the scar. He saw the tiny dot and inhaled her sweet perfume. He almost slipped off the kitchen chair.

Sherry kept talking. "It was a number sixteen Blue Dunn. My parents and I were fishing up by that sheep farm on Portage Creek. There are some great holes along that part of the stream. First, I fell in filling my hipboots with ice water and almost drowned because my stupid parents were laughing so hard they couldn't help me.

"Then I caught my line in about a million bushes. I remember thinking that all I really wanted was a worm and a bobber. I was just about to quit when I stuck the hook in my neck."

Jimmy began to visualize Sherry curled up on her sofa talking on the phone to him as if they had been going together for a long time. She would put her head back when she laughed and run her fingers through her corn silk hair. She would be barefoot and wearing, he couldn't decide, a very long sweatshirt. Maybe it had orange flowers on it, yes, tiger lilies. He did his best to concentrate on listening because that is what his father had told him was important. Listen in the woods, listen to your 'inside voice' he called it, and always listen when women talk. If your response in a conversation, he had said, has nothing to do with what she was saying, she'd know you were drifting. That would signal the beginning of the end.

"Well, I just screamed bloody murder. My dad got the hook out and patted me on the back. 'You gotta expect that, old sport,' he said. Mom and dad thought it would be best if I just sat on the bank and calmed down.

"My dad disappeared downstream. Through teary eyes I watched my mom fish the hole above the bridge, you know, the one that starts with white rapids that flow into a deep, green pool. What I saw was beautiful. It was like she was in a dance, the way her body moved, the way her arms moved, the back and forth sway of the rod with a slight hesitation at the end of each stroke as the line uncurled itself. The sunlight poured through the willow leaves so that the line changed color from green to silver to gold.

"She had on a Blue Winged Olive, a dry fly, which landed at the base of the rapids as gently as a leaf falling and drifted among swirling eddies along the far bank. Suddenly the water exploded! I even remember the rainbow created from the splash. She set the hook and the reel started singing that high whine it makes when the trout runs. The rod was bent, the line cut the water and my mom had a wonderful smile on her face.

"I was next to her when she netted it. It had a rainbow all along its side. I don't remember how long it was, but it was so pretty. She made me wet my hands before I petted it. They have a protective slime on their skin that can be damaged if they are handled wrong. Then, it was so amazing, she let it go. My dad would never do that. I remember clearly sitting on that grassy bank, looking up into my mom's happy face and asking her to teach me to dance like that."

Jimmy said, "That is really cool. Have you written that story in your journal yet?"

"Well, no, I haven't."

"Sherry, if you write that down just as you told it to me, I guarantee that Mr. Fletcher will get the picture."

Sherry and Jimmy laughed together. There was a pause, a lull, then they both tried to speak simultaneously. He said 'you go', and she said 'no, you first'.

"I just think you must be a fine fisherman, I mean woman, ah, girl, person," he fumbled.

"Fisherman is okay. Well, I do have good luck. Would you like to go sometime? Opening day is just two months away,"

"I'd love to, Sherry."

"It's a date then?" she asked.

"A date?" he said before he could call it back.

"Yes. That's what it's called when two people go out and do something together. My mom said it was okay these days for a girl to ask a boy out, especially if he hasn't gotten around to asking her yet."

"Of course, it's fine. It's a date then," he said hearing the slow drum beat in his left temple resume its cadence.

"I'm really glad you called," Sherry said. "I enjoyed it. You're very easy to talk to, Jimmy."

"Thanks. You, too."

"But there is one other thing, Jimmy," Sherry's voice was barely audible like a song you think in your head.

"One thing?" Jimmy said. "What one thing is that?"

"Well, it's good to plan a date a few months ahead, but I think we should do something before then."

"You mean like March?"

"I mean like next weekend," she said as if she were playing out more line.

"You mean like this next week end coming up after this week is over?"

"That's the one. You think about it and we'll talk in school on Monday when I show you my scar, okay?"

"Yes, Monday we'll talk."

"Goodbye, Jimmy."

"Bye, Sherry."

Jimmy hung up the phone and touched his lips as if he had just been kissed there. Sitting alone in the kitchen he stared at the cabinets and said, "Oh, my." Down the hallway he heard Maureen and Sally trying to smother their giggles.

13

A wolf pack establishes a territory for hunting. In order to keep competitors out of their chosen area, they patrol the perimeter sniffing the ground for intruders and scent marking the boundary. Urine sprayed at intervals lets other carnivores know that this part of the forest has already been claimed. Of course, if a prey animal crosses the boundary line, the wolf will follow. I haven't checked on this with a biologist, but I believe that most predation (see thesaurus) occurs within the wolf pack's home range.

It was with this in mind that Hawk and I set out before dawn last Sunday morning for Two Mile Creek. Our goal was to map Romeo's territory by following tracks, locating scat and scent markings (wolf urine must have a very strong smell, pungent says the thesaurus) as well as other signs like kill sites. However, Hawk said that a wolf's territory is generally quite large and it would be impossible for us to hike around it in the time we had. "What a wolf can do in a day," he said, "might take us a week." So we decided to do as much as we could in a day to get an idea of where Romeo hunted.

The cold was brutal. We hiked the old logging road from Lillibridge to the head of Two Mile Creek in the dark. The stars looked like pieces of ice on a black cloth. While we mostly hiked in silence, there was one story Hawk told which explained how the stars came to be. I don't remember it all, but he said something about when man came up out of the earth to live before time was invented, before rivers had names, before trees and rocks even knew what they were, those first human beings looked at an empty sky. There was only darkness each night. At night the darkness was so heavy that men became shadows, ghosts who could no longer see one another. Then the tribes got fire to keep them from turning into ghosts. "As the first human beings got older," Hawk said, "they began to die. The tribes had a hard time thinking of what to make of this. They began to notice after someone passed over to the other world, a single light would appear on the dark blanket of the night sky, which looked from a great distance like a campfire. In fact, that is what they believed then. They believed what they were seeing were campfires from the other world around which their lost elders were sitting wrapped in blankets, smoking their long pipes. Since those first beings, many have died. That is why the sky is so crowded with campfires."

Hawk laughed when he ended the story. He said it was just a story, one his momma used to tell him. She was a good storyteller, he said. Then Hawk said a curious thing that I will have to think about for a long time before I understand it. He said that even though a good story is fiction, is invented in the imagination, it still has to be true. What do you make of that, Mr. Fletcher?

The sky had just a slight stain of light in the east when we reached the creek. Although it hadn't snowed for days, the old snow was still deep. We had to wear the bent oak and deerhide snowshoes we made last winter. Without them we wouldn't have gotten very far.

Because of the snow, the light was very strange. It was as if the snow contained light. The trees were not visible yet, but the snow on them was. The white pines, blue spruce and cedar looked like great mounds of soft white stone. While the branches of the oaks and maples could not be seen, the snow that etched even the tiniest twigs glowed as if suspended in air. The tree smell, the odor of snow and the scent of musk from deer mixed in the air like a natural perfume. The air was still. The woods was silent. Dad was right. This was the same as church.

Hawk said that it was no use sniffing around in the dark so we should just sit for a while. We built a fire and cooked coffee and oatmeal. The sky turned from gray to gold to silver. The forest sparkled with light as if reflected from jewels of many colors. The birds began to talk.

Finally we buried the fire with snow. I waited while Hawk began walking left in a spiral, which is the way you look for sign in order to locate a trail to follow. Within a hundred yards of where we had waited for the sun to rise, Hawk found Romeo's tracks. Even though they were a day old, the tracks were easy to follow. They zigzagged off left into the laurel. Hawk led the way.

I could have done the tracking easily enough because each print was the size of a man's hand, but Hawk was still my teacher. He had more lessons to teach.

The first came when he stopped suddenly and sniffed the air. He looked like a true mountain man in the deer coat he had made for himself with the gray-brown fur on the outside 'like deer wear it' he said. His dark wool pants were tucked into Sorrels and his hands were covered with the rabbit mittens I had made for him. When I had given him the gift, he asked if the rabbit had been inside out before I made the mittens because the fur was on the inside. "I wish I could have seen that rabbit," he said. With his snowshoes on, Hawk looked like someone out of the last century.

Then he sniffed the ground, made an awful face and called me over. I inhaled deeply at the base of a tree stump and nearly fell over. The odor was pure acid, worse than any outhouse I've been in, like roadkill boiled and bloated in the sun. "Wolf scent," Hawk said smiling at my reaction. "What do you suppose he's trying to communicate, Jimmy?"

"I think he's saying 'keep out', but it's a strange way to tell someone something." I was blowing hard through my nose trying to get the smell out. It burned. I could feel the heat on my face.

Hawk laughed his deep belly laugh and said, "If you have the urge to scent mark, it's best you do it outside of Romeo's boundary. We don't want you saying the wrong thing, now do we." And he ambled off down the trail, a great laughing bear.

The trail led through a thick stand of pines where travel was easy for a wolf but very hard for us. At one point Hawk brushed a pine whose upper branches shook. He looked up just as the avalanche of snow found its mark. I asked if he was okay, but I was laughing too hard to help brush him off. He just grumbled something about how I shouldn't laugh at an old man and continued up the trail talking to himself.

Romeo's tracks led through boulder fields, thick patches of green laurel with stiff branches, beds of groundpine and stands of hardwoods. The tracks wandered steadily southeast meandering occasionally to the right or left. By my calculations, we were headed for Old Baldy, which worried me. That hill has very little cover and is used often by hikers and sled riders. It wouldn't be long before Romeo would be discovered.

However, at the Springs where icy water gurgles from a pipe sticking out of stone, Romeo's tracks veered west toward Saddleback and the Rocks. All along the way, Hawk pointed to other tracks in the snow as if he were testing me (the way teachers like to do). I'd say whitetail yearling, or red squirrel or fox or coyote or snowshoe rabbit. For the imprint of a wing in the snow I said Great Horned Owl. He never showed by his facial expression whether he was impressed or not, but his gray-blue eyes gave him away. His student did okay.

Half a mile from the Springs, Hawk stopped and sniffed the air again. After a moment he pointed his mittened hand toward a ridge of gray rocks. We had to climb over several blowdowns in order to reach the spot. Beyond the rocks was a wolf kill, an old buck that had already shed one antler. I counted five points on the other. Locating and studying a kill site was another lesson taught by Hawk.

The viscera, Hawk's term, guts, my term, were gone. Heart, lungs, liver, intestines as well as both hindquarters. Hawk picked up a large black feather. "Raven," he said. "Much more substantial than a crow feather. And here," pointing to a smaller set of tracks, "a bobcat fed last night or this morning. Your wolf feeds many creatures."

I showed Hawk another set of tracks. "Coyote," I said.

"Very big for a coyote, but we do have some around here. He better not let wolf catch him eating his food or wolf will make him sleep by a campfire in the sky."

We felt each of the tracks to tell how old they were. The bobcat's had iced over and were probably from the night before. Romeo's tracks were starting to freeze up which meant that he had been back here just hours before. Hawk said that because the carcass was partially frozen, it had been killed late Friday. The deer's eyes were black glass, its nose buried in the snow. Blood was on its front hooves and the red stain spread out from the body, a dull liquid that had seeped into the trampled snowpack.

"These look to be fresh," I said feeling one of the coyote tracks. "We must have scared her off when we came up the ridge."

"Very big coyote," Hawk said.

I sketched the whole scene in my notebook and drew a partial map of Romeo's territorial border. We started back toward home because it was already late afternoon. The light was low, but the trail was easy to follow. We hadn't gone more than a mile or so when Hawk stopped and turned to me. "You feel it?" he asked. "You feel someone watching us, following us?"

I looked around carefully at the trees, the brush, some rocks protruding through the snow. No one was there. Then we heard it. A sorrowful breath of wind which grew into a sustained howl. I felt a chill. It was mournful like a cry, someone letting go of a lot of sadness. Then again the howl filled the woods, a slightly higher tone, almost an echo of the first. A heartbreak song. Hawk suggested that we build a fire and wait to see if the wolf would show himself.

The fire crackled and spit as yellow-blue flames grew among the kindling sticks. Smoke thin as cold breath rose in a column up through the branches of the maple. We sat with our backs against the wide tree trunk. The sun had fallen into the lap of the far mountains. The woods had turned gray as if everything were covered with ash.

We sat for what seemed a long time listening, smelling the air, peering into the disappearing woods. Hawk tapped my shoulder. I looked at him and followed his gaze through the woodsmoke to a line of cedars. At the base of one tree stood the black wolf. He was standing sideways, as I had first seen him with his great head turned toward us. He was so close I could see twin campfires burning in his yellow eyes. "Stay still," Hawk whispered. "He doesn't know me yet. With this coat on, he may think I'm dinner."

Romeo held his head erect but his tail low. Then he sat and whined, just a whimper. Then he lay down with his head still erect. He was a huge animal. In that dim light, he might have easily been mistaken for a bear. I could see the fur around his barrel chest rise and fall as he breathed.

Hawk began to talk to the wolf in a quiet voice. He said, "Wolf, I am Hawk. You are a great mystery to us because we know your blood remembers the past, and still you come and share our fire. What have young Jimmy and I done to deserve such a gift?"

Romeo's ears twitched at the sound of Hawk's voice. Then he stood but did not leave. He looked along the row of cedar trunks. Hawk touched my shoulder again and said, "Those weren't coyote tracks we found." He pointed to the left. Standing there in the thin light like a luminous dream vision was a white female wolf. There was enough light to see gray streaks along her cheeks and the top ridge of her tail. She held her head erect, her thick tail straight out. Her eyes were every bit as intense as her mate's, and when she looked at me, they had the same fire.

I knew that the movement I had seen the last time Romeo came to my fire was this beautiful wolf whose coloration had made her invisible. She looked back at Romeo and then at us again. The thick fur along her neck had a pearlish tint to it. I could see that there was some gray along her back too. Her nose, like a piece of coal, was sugared with snow. She appeared like a snowdrift with a face. She moved next to Romeo, licked his face, and sat next to him watching us.

My emotions were in chaos. I wanted to laugh. I wanted to cry. All I could manage to do in the weakest of whispers was say, "Juliet."

14

Jimmy stumbled into English class, his nerves like a bag of live snakes wriggling in his stomach. He couldn't wait to see Sherry. He dreaded seeing her. Once in his seat, panic set in. If only I could be out hiking a mountain ridge, he thought, or getting hopelessly lost in some remote valley. Damp hands wiped against pant legs. A muscle knotted in his neck.

Sherry came into the room with several of her girlfriends. Her friends smiled at Jimmy as they took their seats. They knew, he thought. Sherry moved down his row past her seat and said, "Hi, Jimmy. Can I show you my scar?"

"May I," said Mr. Fletcher who was standing in front of the bulletin board in the back of the room trying to hang a poster which quoted a William Carlos Williams poem superimposed over a photograph of a wheelbarrow in a farmyard full of white chickens.

"May I?" Sherry repeated making a funny face.

"Oh, yea, sure," Jimmy whispered feeling suddenly calm.

Sherry stooped close to Jimmy and, with a toss of her head, flicked her hair back so that the tips brushed his face. With her left hand she held her golden hair aside exposing her neck. And there it was, a small, white dot like a period in the middle of a beautiful sentence. Jimmy stared at the tiny scar aware of the bouquet of perfume encircling him like a snare.

"That must have hurt," he said.

Sherry grimaced remembering the hook. "It hurt worse coming out than going in. Barbed hooks are like that. You can touch it if you like."

His fingers moved along the back of Sherry's neck over the scar. The minute bump, like a single Braille mark, sent many messages along the intricate wires of Jimmy's nerves. He withdrew his hand afraid that he had left it there too long.

"Your hand is cold," she said turning to face him.

"That's strange," he said. "They were just sweating a few minutes ago."

Sherry's green eyes were hypnotic jewels. Jimmy was caught in their spell. "Will you sit with me at lunch," she said, "so we can talk about our, you know, plan?"

"Yes, lunch, I will," he said wishing he could get out more of a sentence.

"See you then," she said moving up to her seat.

Jimmy never heard a word Fletcher said that period. He did listen intently when Sherry read her fly fishing journal entry. He felt privileged already knowing each sentence before she uttered it. He began to sense an intimate connection with the dream girl in the second row, third seat. The feeling had started to grow Saturday night when, on the phone, they had trusted each other with their words.

Class ended. Chattering students crowded through the door into the hall. Sherry touched Jimmy's shoulder. "See you at lunch," she smiled.

'Tis twenty years till then,' Jimmy thought, then said aloud, "Yes, lunch."

"I see you brought your lunch," Sherry said placing her tray on the table and sitting next to Jimmy on the bench. He was immediately aware that their sitting together sent a message that moved like a bird spreading gossip from table to table. Eyes turned. Whispers could be heard. Jimmy didn't care. He was with Sherry. That was all that mattered to him.

"I always bring my lunch. My mother says that the chemistry class should test the cafeteria food to see if they can find any sign of nutrition." Two sentences, he thought to himself, good start.

"Good idea. Just look at this mystery meat in gravy. I usually only eat the fries and fruit. And the milk, of course. It's hard to mess up milk." Sherry was close enough that their arms touched. Neither moved away.

Jimmy swallowed a bite of his meatloaf sandwich, took a drink from his water bottle and said, "Your journal entry this morning was really good. You read it so well, too. The whole time I was thinking of the scar on your neck."

Sherry smiled and leaned against him. "I couldn't have done it without your help. I was getting so frustrated. Everything I tried to write seemed so dull. You taught me to see, to see what was important beyond the facts. Then the writing was easy, more natural."

"Do you remember Miss Fisk?" he said.

"Yes. Seventh grade art teacher. I was so bad at drawing."

Jimmy smiled and continued, "Well, she was always saying 'draw what *you* want, not what *I* want.' What she meant, I think, was not to guess what other people want, not to try to please others, but paint and draw what pleased us. Writing is the same way. I started my first journal that year by writing in my sketchbook details about the animals and plants I drew. The first drawing I did was of an owl's wing. Then I wrote next to it about how the fine feathers along the front of the wing muffled the sound of flight so that the owl was able to approach its prey in total silence. It made me happy to write that. Miss Fisk seemed to like it, too. I'm sorry; I shouldn't be talking so much."

"Oh, no, I love listening to you talk," Sherry said. "Maybe I could illustrate some of my journal entries, draw reels, rods, flies and stuff like that. Unfortunately, the only thing I can draw well is a dead tree. I'll have to practice the fishing stuff."

A parade of people carrying trays of food passed their table, each saying 'Hello, Sherry' in slow, drawn out voices that indicated they knew what was going on between the two of them.

"Don't mind them," Sherry said, "they're just jealous."

"I don't mind. I really don't know most of those kids very well. I guess because I live on the farm, I don't get to know many people."

"You mean you're a loner, a lone wolf." She smiled again as did Jimmy. What pleasure it was, he thought, to listen to her watery voice, to look into those sparkling green eyes and to inhale her scent, a fragrance that made him dizzy. He would be content to do this for the rest of the day, for the rest of his life.

"So," Sherry said, "what about Saturday? What would you like to do?" Her gaze was intense.

"Well, I'm sort of new at this. We could go to a movie."

"The only problem with that," Sherry grinned, "is that the theater closed last year."

"Oh, it did?" Jimmy felt embarrassed. "I didn't know. What would you like to do?"

"Well, if you don't have to work, I would love to go on a hike. It wouldn't cost us anything. My dad said he could drop me off in the morning. We could go up in the woods behind your house. You could show me all you're secret places and teach me how to track. I'd really like to see the woods through your eyes. I want to see where your imaginary wolf lives." Sherry put down her milk carton and placed her hand on Jimmy's arm. He moved his hand to hers.

In the deep recesses of his mind an alarm sounded, something about Romeo and now Juliet and betraying their isolated world to the warden's daughter. But he ignored it.

"Are you sure? You know it's February. The cold is bone chilling and the snow is so deep. It wouldn't be easy."

"I'm used to it!" she said. "I've been cross-country skiing for years. The colder, the better."

"I don't have skis, but I have two pairs of snowshoes. Would that be okay?"

"Perfect," she smiled, "if you'll teach me how to walk in them."

"Sure I will. You just move the right foot forward and then the left."

Sherry squeezed Jimmy's arm just as the bell rang signaling the end of lunch. Jimmy did not want to move his hand from hers.

"It's a date then?" Sherry asked.

"Yes, a date," Jimmy whispered.

15

wj 27 February

In social studies we've been talking about prejudice, about how throughout history there have been groups of people who have tried to exterminate other groups of people because they were different in appearance or beliefs. Mr. Burns said prejudice is 'born of ignorance and fear'. Through the whole discussion, I've been thinking about the wolf.

Wolves have been shot, poisoned and trapped because of 'ignorance and fear'. If we could erase those two things, the wolf could survive, reclaim its place in the natural world, restore balance to the environment from which it has been removed. Without the wolf, the coyote population has increased. Although they will prey on deer, coyotes prefer smaller animals such as squirrels, rabbits, beaver. As a result, those populations have decreased reducing the food source for foxes, eagles, hawks and owls, which in turn impacts their numbers.

What I'm trying to say is that all things are connected. My friend Hawk is always talking about the web of life as he calls it. The spider, he says, will eat well if he weaves a good web. If he doesn't, he starves. Hawk said that the wolf evolved as part of Nature's plan. Without the wolf, the plan isn't very good. Other animals depend on him to make them strong, to keep their numbers in check.

If more people understood the ways of the wolf, their 'ignorance and fear' would subside. They would see the important role it plays in the over all scheme of things, see that it is not an enemy, but a brother which is how Hawk sees the wolf. He told me once that the bigger problem is that man no longer sees himself as a part of the natural order of things, but separate from it, that nature is there to serve man's needs. He says that arrogance and disrespect were the bullets and poison that killed the wolf.

At dinner last night my father asked Hawk to tell the story of the three-legged wolf. It was a story Hawk had heard from his father who had heard it from his father.

A farmer found wolf tracks in mud by a stream, which flowed through his pasture. They were big tracks. Even though the wolf hadn't harmed any cattle, the farmer hired a wolfer, someone whose occupation it was to kill wolves, to find and eliminate this one.

The wolfer was a grizzly old guy, hard as rock, expressionless face, eyes like two stones. The man gave off a wild odor like rotting meat. The saddle blanket on his gray horse was really a wolf skin. The man set off to track the wolf.

For days he followed the wolf's trail through dense woods, edging along mountain cliffs and descending into valley fields and swamps. He studied the animal's territory until it became his own. Then he set his traps. He smeared elk blood on six steel tooth, leg traps and buried them in a circle under earth and leaves on a trail he knew this wolf traveled every few days. A seventh trap was staked in the center of the circle and baited with an elk heart and liver.

All of this was done, Hawk said, to kill an animal that hadn't even done any harm. When the wolfer returned several days later, he discovered that one of the traps had been sprung. It still held the wolf's foot, but the wolf was gone.

The wolfer told the farmer that he had seen that before with raccoons and foxes. "He won't last long," the wolfer smiled. "Lost too much blood." The farmer refused to pay him until he brought back the carcass.

Weeks went by with no sign of the wolf or the wolfer. The farmer's little daughter told him one morning that she had had a dream about the wolf. It was limping through the woods. She was walking beside it. She said it didn't feel like a scary dream. In the dream she felt safe.

Working in the barn that afternoon, the farmer heard the panicked cries of his daughter. She was wading in the shallow stream, which flowed along the far edge of the pasture. Twenty yards from her, a black bear had reared up snarling and was pawing wildly at the air. Even though the farmer knew he could not get there in time, he started running toward the terrified girl.

The bear, a huge male, dropped onto all fours and charged at the child. When it reached the creek bank, a gray streak shot from nearby bushes and crashed into the bear rolling it over and drawing blood from its neck. While the two animals thrashed and snarled in the brush, the farmer snatched up his daughter and retreated to safety. The farmer saw that it was the three-legged wolf that had attacked the bear. It continued to harass the animal as it stumbled toward the woods. Finally, the bear ran off looking back often to make sure the wolf was no longer in pursuit. The wolf sat for a while licking fresh blood from its coat. Then, as suddenly as he had appeared, he was gone, hidden by the thick green brush along the stream.

That night the wolfer returned. The farmer paid him and said that his job was done. The wolfer said, "No carcass, no pay." The farmer said that he and his daughter had found the wolf and that it would no longer be a problem. The wolfer left.

Hawk said that the farmer never saw the wolf again, never found tracks along the creek. But the wolf often visited his daughter, at night, in her dreams. They would walk all the trails in his territory. She would follow; he would limp ahead. Hawk added, "Of course, this is just a story."

Sometimes I feel very sad when I think that if Romeo and Juliet were real wolves, ignorance and fear, arrogance and disrespect would harm them as it has so many others, wolves and people.

16

When he heard the truck door close, Jimmy looked out the kitchen window. Sherry, wearing a blue parka and white ski pants, was walking toward the house. Her father slid out of the dark green Ford. Jimmy pulled on his jacket and went out onto the porch to meet her. The screen door banged behind him.

"Good morning, Mr. Woolman," he called.

"Same to you, Jimmy," Woolman said.

"Hi," he said more softly to Sherry who bounded up the steps pulling off her white knit cap. Her long hair danced like summer wheat in a windy field. She smiled and gave him a hug. Jimmy felt embarrassed having her do that in front of her dad.

Woolman climbed the stairs. "Now you two wont go too far, will ya? There's a storm comin' in tonight. We got a few inches already."

"Don't worry, Mr. Woolman, we're just going to hike over that ridge to the head of Two Mile." Jimmy pointed up Lillibridge Creek toward a line where the white hill and the gray sky met.

"It'll be okay, daddy," Sherry said holding onto Jimmy's arm, "I'll be in good hands."

"Well, yes, I suppose so, but your mother and I still worry. I'll be back from Smethport along about dark. Make sure you're back by then."

"Yes, daddy, we will, promise."

"We'll be here, Mr. Woolman, " Jimmy said.

Jimmy's parents came out onto the porch. "Mornin', Woolman," Joe said.

"Let me pour you a cup of coffee, just made it fresh," said Martha.

"I sure would like that, but I gotta get over to the office. Had a few bear complaints come in last night. I think they're all from the same bear. He's probably the one I relocated last year for squeezing garbage cans. Seems partial to chasing cats, too. We took him way over to the national forest the other side of Bradford. More room for him over there, but I bet he found his way back."

Joe said, "Maybe we got a higher class of garbage here than they got over there. You need any help? I sure would like to get out of doin' chores today."

"Well, I could use a hand locating the critter if you wanna come along."

"Jimmy here could find him in no time, but he seems to be booked up for the day." Joe winked at Sherry. "I'll get my coat and boots. Be right with you." Joe went inside, Martha followed. She came back with a cup of steaming coffee that she handed to Woolman.

"You take it black, Fred?" she asked.

"Yes, thanks," said Woolman sipping. "Tastes real good on a raw day like this one. I told the kids I'd be back come dark. Is that okay with you?"

"They'll be fine. I expect they'll return in a couple of hours. When it gets this cold, it's hard to stay away from the woodstove."

"I'm ready," said Joe emerging from the house buttoning his red and black plaid hunting coat. His wool pants were tucked into the fur snowguard of his sorrel boots. "You kids behave today. No snowball fights and no unnecessary laughing. I'll see you tonight, sweet." Joe kissed Martha on the cheek.

Woolman handed his cup back to Martha and said, "See you all later."

Snow swirled around the truck as it bumped along the drive to the main road. Martha turned to Sherry. "My goodness, we haven't even said good morning to you yet. Where are my manners? You come right in here now, Sherry. Warm blueberry muffins will be just the fuel to help you up that hill."

Wearing snowshoes, Jimmy and Sherry moved awkwardly upstream along the creek bank. Steam rose from the dark water, which churned over rounded stones making soft sounds like whispering voices. She held onto his arm for balance. Twice they stepped on each other's shoes causing them both to tumble into the snow. They laughed and laughed and threw snow at each other like two children playing. Finally, Sherry was able to walk on her own, and they made good time on the creek trail which led up the hillside into the woods where trees stood stark and leafless against the white ground.

A light snow fell on their tracks. Jimmy was warm with excitement. This was his woods, the place where he felt most comfortable. He was pleased to share it with Sherry. She seemed so happy, he thought, so pretty, so interested in everything, especially him. Maybe he could trust her with his secret, with Romeo and Juliet. He decided to see how the day went. Maybe he'd tell her later, maybe not.

Even though the trail was steep, they made it to the wolf site within a few hours. Along the way Jimmy translated the tracks they encountered into stories of what had happened earlier that morning. He showed her tiny mouse tracks that ended in a small clearing among multiple imprints of wings. Coopers Hawk, he had said. Poor mouse, she said. He showed her fresh deer tracks and told their ages. He explained how the bacteria in the whitetail's stomach changes during the winter to digest woody material allowing them to eat twigs. Deer who are fed straw in winter could die of starvation with full stomachs because they cannot digest the food, he had said.

"All this talk is making me hungry," Sherry said placing her backpack on a fallen log. "Can we build a fire and have some lunch?"

"I'll get some wood. You can stomp around here and pack this snow down."

While Jimmy collected dry sticks, he kept looking back at Sherry. Here was a girl, he thought, who, rather than being in a movie theater eating popcorn or sitting in a booth at the Maplewood Diner sipping cocoa, was content to be in the snowy woods having lunch with him by a campfire. He watched her jump up and down. She looked like a little kid hopping in a mud puddle. Sherry saw him watching and smiled. She was really something, he thought.

Snowflakes fell hissing into the yellow flames. Gray smoke rose above the mountain laurel and drifted east through barren maples and oaks to a stand of cedars where it disappeared. Jimmy and Sherry sat on a wool blanket and leaned back against a log and each other. They ate peanut butter and jelly sandwiches and drank tea, which Sherry had brought along. At first neither spoke much. Their attention was focused on the dancing flames, the falling snow, the green of the laurel bushes, the intricate weave of branches like a web catching the white flakes.

When they did speak, they did so simultaneously.

"Do you hear . . .", Sherry said.

"Do you hear . . .", Jimmy said. "Oh, I'm sorry. You go ahead."

Sherry smiled. "I was just going to ask you if you hear what I hear."

"You mean the silence?"

"Yes," she said turning to him.

"That's what I was going to say. Other than the fire crackling, there isn't a sound. I feel badly sometimes for those kids at school who wear headphones all the time. With all that noise in your head, there isn't any room for your own thoughts to grow. That's why I like it up here. No distractions. It's easy to think in a place like this."

"What do you think about, Jimmy?" Sherry said, the breath of her words mingled with the breath of his words both of which hung in the air momentarily before dissipating.

"Well, I think about," he said slowly, "the things that I've learned, the pictures I've drawn and the things I want to write about. I think a lot about what Hawk has taught me, all the stories he tells. He always says they're just stories, but I know he thinks they're true."

"What stories?"

"He told me how the stars came to be, about the medicine wheel, the *Going Away Tale* I wrote about in my first journal entry, the smoke ceremony, how to make an offering. I put all of those in my journal. It helps me to remember, to understand."

"Could I read your journal some day?" Sherry asked. "It must be so interesting, and you didn't even mention wolves yet."

"You can read it now, if you like. I have it in my pack. It's with me all the time." Jimmy pulled the journal from his pack and handed it to her. She ran her hand over the leather cover, removed her glove traced the image of the wolf feeling the slight indent of the burned lines. Jimmy knelt by the fire feeding it with dead sticks.

"Writing things in there," he said, "has helped me notice details more, you know, like the trails on this stick left by insects eating the wood while the bark was still on." He held it up for her to see. "They're like clues to what happened. It tells a story, a small story, but all the small stories make up a bigger story. After a while you begin to realize that one story could not happen without the others. Does that make any sense?"

"I think so. Can I read this out loud, Jimmy?"

"Sure, go ahead."

He settled down beside her as she began reading:

On our farm my sisters and I help my parents with all the chores in order to make the farm work successfully. Everyone has his own responsibilities. Each member of the family contributes to the success of the farm, which is our livelihood.

The same is true for wolves . . .

Sherry continued reading entry after entry. Jimmy loved hearing his words spoken by her. He could actually feel the bond between them growing in strength. The notes of her voice were like strings connecting them to one another, each sentence a separate strand. Even when she came to a line written to reassure Mr. Fletcher that this story was fiction after which she looked at him, he felt no panic. He knew now that he would tell her the truth. In his mind he had already begun to compose the words that would lead to it.

Sherry brushed snowflakes from each page as she read on into the afternoon. When she got to the end of the entry where Juliet appeared, she closed the journal and leaned her head on Jimmy's shoulder.

"Jimmy," she whispered, "your story is so beautiful, so real, I feel as though I was with you and Romeo and Juliet."

Jimmy watched the flames caress the thick sticks. He watched the smoke rise. After a moment he said, "There is something I need to tell you, Sherry. Hawk told me a story recently about how the ancestors believed that wolf and man came together over a hundred centuries ago. They call wolf brother because of the bond created back then. Man provided food and fire. The wolf, with its keen senses of smell, hearing and sight, gave protection and assisted with the hunt. Hawk said that people today think that *we* domesticated the wolf. He said the elders believed the *wolf* chose us. He is the one who came to our campfire. I don't know if that is true, but Hawk thinks that is what has happened up here."

Sherry lifted her head and looked at Jimmy. Her face was serious, puzzled. "What do you mean 'up here'?" she said.

Jimmy drew in a long breath and smiled. "Hawk thinks the wolves, Romeo and Juliet, chose me."

Sherry looked confused.

"I've been wanting to tell you, but their safety depends on keeping their presence here a secret. You can't let anyone know, especially your father."

"Know? Know what?"

"The wolves I've been writing about in my journal aren't fiction. Everything you read today actually happened. You see that pine bough drooping over the laurel? There's the medicine bag I left as an offering. It still has the coins, the corn kernels, the grass and bark in it."

"You mean you saw wolves right here?" Sherry moved closer to Jimmy. "Weren't you scared they might do something?"

"You don't have to worry. They mean no harm. Hawk thinks they haven't experienced the brutality that once wiped them out of here. He says they're as innocent as I am. So they trust the way I trust you with their secret. If you feel uncomfortable, we can head back. Besides, it's beginning to snow harder. We should probably get going."

"Oh, I don't want to leave yet. I'm okay, really. It's just so hard to believe. Everything I know about wolves came from movies and kids' stories. But if you say it's okay, then it is."

Sherry snuggled down next to Jimmy. He held her close. They were quiet for a while. The snow fell silently on the branches, the laurel, the forest floor, the fire. Quiet moved in around them like a blanket, a white cloth.

"Could we try the smoke ceremony?" Sherry finally asked.

Jimmy knew then that not only had she accepted the truth of the secret, she would keep it.

"Yes," he said brushing snow from her hair.

17

wj 7 March

*L*ast night I had a strange dream. It reminded me of Hawk's story about how the wolves spoke to his ancestors in dreams. In my dream I was running, not from anything, just for the joy of it. It was a cool summer morning. The red sun had risen over the distant peaks of the Alleghenies. I was moving along a bare ridge following a deer trail.

I descended into the woods where the underbrush was thick. Thin branches slapped against me as I rushed along the path. The scent of earth, pine, flower and fungus mixed together to form a strong perfume. I felt so alive, alert.

As I moved, I noticed flashes of black to my left and flashes of white to my right. Then I could hear their breathing. Romeo and Juliet were loping along beside me.

We entered a clearing in a high valley. It was strewn with old, fallen trees covered with moss. Clusters of wild flowers surrounded each log. I leapt the hurdles one at a time. The wolves cleared each together as if they were one wolf, their muscles flexing and relaxing, graceful in their gait.

A spring flowed down a slope to a flat piece of woods where it pooled in a wide rock bowl struck with shafts of sunlight. There we rested. The wolves drank, their long tongues lapping the cool water. I got down on my hands and knees and drank, too. Their eyes watched me. I studied their reflection in the pool. It was as if I was looking through them to the bottom. Their fur was a mat of brown leaves. Their eyes, two pairs of gold stars floating on the water.

This was not one of those really weird dreams where I become a wolf. In this dream, I was myself, so close to the wild, so connected to my own animal nature, a part of us that has been lost, tamed. There have been people, recluses, who have dared to stay in the wild, living on its terms, who have written of this. Hawk said it was an essential experience among his people, especially for young ones coming of age. Out of it grew respect for the earth, and out of that grew respect for the self, which is part of the earth.

Maybe that was what Romeo and Juliet were trying to tell me in this dream. Not that I am one of them, but that I am part of what they are part of. We are linked, both born of the same ground, both drinking from the same pool.

18

*S*herry built up the fire with small sticks while Jimmy cut fresh pine boughs. He placed the green branches on the fire. They crackled and snapped giving off a cloud of gray-white smoke that rose in a straight column.

"Sit here by me," Jimmy said pointing to a spot of trodden snow next to the fire. They sat together. "I have a gift for you. It isn't much, just something I made." From his pocket he pulled a necklace, strips of dark leather braided together. Woven into the center were two smooth stones, one black, one white. He brushed her hair back and tied the necklace in place.

"It's so perfect, Jimmy."

"Now watch what I do, then you try." Sherry looked on as Jimmy cupped his hands, pulled the smoke to his chest and guided it over his face. He did this several times before turning to her. "It's best, of course, to close your eyes and not breathe in. Go ahead, see what happens."

Sherry put her hands together, took a deep breath and pulled the smoke toward her. She began to cough and fall backward away from the smoke. "I'm sorry," she gasped.

"It's okay. Here, try again."

She repeated the ceremony guiding the smoke up over her head. Jimmy smiled, "That's good! You can breathe now."

Sherry blew out hard and sucked in cold air. "Whew!" she said. "Is that all there is to it?"

"There's more. Hawk says it helps to say words that come from your own heart, but what I do is try to visualize the wolves coming through the woods toward me. It doesn't always work, but a few times it has."

"Let's do it together," Sherry said. "You think of Romeo and I'll picture Juliet. Will that work?"

"It might, but don't be disappointed if it doesn't. They may well be bedded down somewhere because of the snow."

"We can try at least," she whispered, her green eyes bright with excitement.

They both closed their eyes and began pulling the smoke in, guiding it over their bodies, their heads. They moved slowly, deliberately. The movement of their arms seemed to beckon whatever was hidden in the falling snow, in the dense woods beyond to draw near.

In his imagination Jimmy saw the black wolf lifting its great head as if it were listening to voices on the wind. He watched it step through deep snow as it moved among the gray tree trunks appearing and disappearing, flashes of black like in the dream he had had.

Sherry tried to picture the white wolf, snow on its muzzle, white dust along its gray back. She, too, saw Juliet moving, stepping over fallen limbs, and brushing snow from laurel as she passed. Sherry could hear the muffled sound of water flowing under ice. Juliet crossed a spring and slipped behind a curtain of pine trees whose branches drooped with their white burden.

Time passed. Snow continued to fall. Jimmy placed more wood and pine boughs on the fire. Both sat still without speaking, eyes closed, their minds focused on the vision within.

After a long while, Jimmy broke the silence. "It doesn't always work, Sherry," he apologized.

She whispered, "I could actually see her. She was moving this way. I'm certain Juliet is near."

"Even if she is close by," he said, "we might not see her because of the snow. It's really coming down now. We better be on our way, Sherry."

Sherry was looking through the column of gray smoke into the milk white fog of the falling snow. Jimmy's voice was a distant hum, barely audible. He sat closer to her, put his arm around her and began to urge her to move when she pointed toward the laurel.

"There," she said softly. "There."

Jimmy saw the white form move near the bushes. Her chalky coat blended so well with the powdery drifts that he had to blink in order to be sure he was seeing what he was seeing. Juliet moved to the right and stood facing them. Then, like a black shadow, Romeo came up behind her and stood statue still.

Sherry gasped. "Shhh," whispered Jimmy. "Now you know. You see how their tails are lowered. That means they aren't nervous about us. Look at those eyes!"

Through the falling snow, their yellow eyes shown, piercing, intense, alive. Sherry clenched Jimmy's arm tightly. "Romeo and Juliet," she said softly. "I can't believe it. Are you sure this isn't part of what I was seeing in my head?"

"They're real enough," he said.

The wolves did not stay long. They rubbed muzzles together and licked each other. Juliet looked off in several directions as if she were picking up inaudible signals from the deep woods. Romeo sniffed the air, reading the story the wind was telling. Then they shook snow from their thick coats and vanished like so much smoke dissipating in the milk of the sky.

Jimmy and Sherry looked at each other, their faces just inches apart, the steam of their breath mixing. Sherry's cheeks were red from the cold, her green eyes alive with light. Without hesitation Jimmy leaned closer pressing his lips to hers. A warm wave rolled through him, through her. They held each other for a long moment not wanting to part, not wanting to let go of all they had discovered about each other, about themselves.

Jimmy pulled back slightly. "We better go," he whispered. "It's very late. We'll have a hard time getting back by dark in all this snow."

Sherry's eyes were barely open. "Yes, we better," she said closing her eyes pulling him to her. Their lips met again. Thick snowflakes hissed in the fire. Wind swirled smoke around them. They both began to cough, then laugh. "Come on, we gotta go," she said.

Jimmy smothered the fire with snow while Sherry loaded the backpacks. They strapped on snowshoes and, holding hands, headed down the creek trail.

The wind strengthened. The snow intensified. Visibility vanished. Light began to fade. Jimmy followed the trail from memory. He moved from tree to tree shuffling along holding Sherry's hand tightly. The whiteout made the terrain foreign. The moaning wind was ominous. Branches clacked together above them and tree trunks squeaked under the weight of the wind.

"Are we lost yet?" shouted Sherry.

"Not yet," Jimmy reassured her. "As long as we're descending, we should be okay. I'll let you know when it's time to worry."

She smiled shivering slightly. They moved on slowly through the swirling snow. Several times Sherry slipped and fell. Each time Jimmy pulled her upright, brushed her off, and continued on. She did not complain. After a while Jimmy began to feel pangs of doubt. We should be very near home by now, he thought. Then he would see a burl like a bowl on the side of a maple tree or a broken trunk, which were familiar landmarks.

When they rested, he reassured her that they were on the right trail. "The thing is," he said loudly, "we're just not making good time. It'll be well after dark before we get back. Your dad will just have to understand."

"I wasn't thinking about him. I was thinking about the wolves. I hope they're all right," she said.

"They love this stuff. They're much better in this weather than we are. You doing okay?"

"Yes!" she said shakily. "We can keep going."

Daylight dimmed and went out. Jimmy moved more cautiously testing each step. The beam of his penlight was faint, almost useless in the white blur. Signs that he could follow in daylight were no longer visible. He proceeded mostly on instinct relying on an internal map to guide him through the geography that was so much a part of him.

He shouted over the wind, "You're one tough girl, Sherry! Anyone else would've been whining the whole way. Some date, huh?"

"I wouldn't have missed it for anything," she said. "I hope my father's not too worried."

"He probably is. We can't do anything about that though. Let's keep going."

They moved on awkwardly through the dark storm. Snow crystals struck their faces like cinders being tossed on the wind. Jimmy led them through a boulder field into a stand of pines. Each pine was a tower of snow whose top disappeared in the churning white chaos above. Standing together, the towers formed an impenetrable wall. Jimmy could not see a way through. The deep snow and the dark night made the place strange to him.

He turned to Sherry who was holding his arm tightly. "If you want to, you could start worrying a little now. I'm just not sure about this place. We can't be too far off the trail though."

She put her face close to his so that he could hear her. "We have another problem, Jimmy," Sherry said, her voice like ice cracking. "I can't get warm. My whole body's shaking. My face is freezing. I can't feel my feet. My fingers won't bend. They feel like needle pricks all over. I'm sorry. I didn't want to complain."

He held her arm for a moment and felt the trembling. Hypothermia, he thought, we've got to stop. He said to her, "It's gotten much colder. The snowflakes are smaller, harder. The windchill is well below zero. We better find some shelter and take cover for a while. Try to get warmed up."

"That sounds good to me, " she stammered.

Jimmy removed one of his snowshoes. His right leg sunk into the snow up to his knee. He struggled to extricate himself and gradually moved to the base of one of the pines. Using the snowshoe as a shovel, he dug away at the deep powder. With each swipe, an avalanche of new powder rushed down from the upper branches filling the space he had cleared. He removed that as well. Jimmy kept digging until one branch was free. It lifted several feet creating a low roof over a tunnel entrance. He removed his other snowshoe and crawled into the hole. Shortly, he emerged looking like a wild animal slithering from its cave.

"Come on," he shouted. "This will work fine!"

"Are you sure?"

"I didn't see any bears sleeping in there. Go on in and see."

Sherry removed her snowshoes, peered into the dark hole and tentatively slid in on her belly dragging the shoes behind her. Jimmy crawled in, too. He switched his pen light back on and propped it against the tree trunk so that its thin ray illuminated the green and white canopy above. He had scraped snow from the cave floor exposing a bed of dry needles. They used their snowshoes as cushions. Jimmy removed the wool blanket from his pack and wrapped it around Sherry.

"There," he said, "that'll trap your body heat. Here, drink some water." He held his thermos cup up to her lips. She sipped shakily. "Eat some of these. You'll need the fuel." He offered her a brown bag with a half dozen chocolate chip cookies. "And put these fleece gloves on under your mittens. We'll get you warm in no time," he reassured her. "Let me take off your boots and socks. If we can get your feet warm, you'll feel much better." He unlaced each boot and tugged them off. He pulled off her socks. "Your feet are like ice." Jimmy rubbed one rapidly with both hands, then the other. Then the first. "This isn't helping much." He lay down in front of her and pulled up is jacket, shirt, thermals and undershirt exposing his white stomach. "Put your feet right here, both of them. This'll do the trick." Sherry obeyed. Jimmy pulled his clothing back down covering her feet and ankles. "Just keep them right there. Can you feel anything?"

Sherry nodded and said weakly, "Yes, but aren't you cold, Jimmy?"

"It's okay. We've got to get your circulation moving. Try rubbing your hands and moving your arms around. Keep your feet right there. What happens when you trudge through snow like that is you sweat a lot, then the sweat cools. The body keeps losing heat it can't replace. Water, food and rest help warm you up. Believe it or not, all this snow around us acts as insulation from the really cold air out there. Down at the Smith Library there's a trapper's journal. He wrote about getting lost in a blizzard. He survived by burrowing into a snow bank and sleeping until the storm passed."

"This is like being in an igloo," Sherry said. "Look up there."

Above, the dark barked branches, thick as wrists, sparred out from the trunk. Each spread like a green fan above which compressed snow was visible in the thin light. It was as if the two were sitting at the bottom of a shaft, the top of which could not be seen. The base of their cave was ten feet across with green walls leaning in.

They rested for a long while. Sherry ate the cookies and sipped the remaining water. Eventually, she began to wiggle her toes and said, "I'm much better, Jimmy. I can feel my feet."

Jimmy sat up, tucked in his shirts and zipped his coat. "I have fresh socks in my pack. Yours are still wet. Let me put these on you. The blue ones are undersocks, like underwear for your feet." He slipped each one on and rubbed her feet gently for a few minutes. "They wick moisture away from your skin. These wool socks will help keep the heat in. Now your boots." He laced each one snugly and sat next to her.

"Why do you have so many socks with you?" Sherry asked, her voice clear, more steady.

"I'm always falling in creeks or stepping in swamps. Getting wet in the woods, even in good weather, is never good. I'm glad you're feeling more comfortable. Hypothermia can be dangerous if you don't take care of it right away. It helps, too, if we stay real close together like this." He put his arm around her. "This way my body heat will help keep you warm."

"Was that in the trapper's journal, too?" Sherry said. "It sounds like something you'd make up, a real smooth line."

"Oh, no. It's true. I swear!"

Sherry smiled in the dim light and extended the blanket around Jimmy. They huddled together listening to the howling storm. Trees cracked and groaned like ghost voices. Clumps of snow occasionally thumped the ground near the entrance. The air was thick with pine scent.

"I don't suppose we could build a fire?" Sherry said.

"Remember that Jack London story we read in Mr. Fletcher's class?"

"Oh, yes. Things didn't work out too well for that guy. How cold do you think it is?"

"Very."

"My father's going to kill me," she said.

"I don't think so. He'll understand. It's all my fault anyway. I'll make sure he knows that."

"What I mean is," Sherry whispered, "he just doesn't like for me to stay over night on the first date."

They looked at one another wide eyed and began to laugh.

"Yea, I can see how he might be upset, but it just can't be helped," Jimmy smiled.

"How late do you think it is?"

"Around eight or nine, but it could be later."

"Do you think, Jimmy, they'll come looking for us?"

"Probably. I don't know how far we are from the logging road. If we hear snowmobiles, we can head that way. For now, we just have to keep warm and get our strength back."

"I've stopped shivering."

"Me, too."

They fell silent for a long while. The dark voices of the storm seemed to grow muffled, more distant. The wind was staying up in the sky brushing the mountaintop. Silence moved in quiet as thought. They listened.

"Sherry, you awake?"

"Yes. I was just daydreaming. Can you daydream at night?"

"I think so."

"I was just thinking about Romeo and Juliet. They were so beautiful. It's hard to believe that they are up there, that we saw them. Her coat was so white, so thick. I think both of them talked with their eyes. They talk feelings, not words." Sherry sighed. "I'm sure they're both curled up together in a safe place just like we are."

"Shhh! Listen," Jimmy whispered. "Did you hear that?"

"What?"

"Just listen."

At first there was nothing except the high rushing of the wind. Then there was a distant noise like rock striking rock. Then again. A long pause. Again. Closer this time. Metal against rock. Then a branch off in the dark snapped like a bone breaking. Then silence.

"What is that?" Sherry huddled even closer to Jimmy.

A string of rhythmic bass notes like an owl call reached them, followed by another the same as the first.

"An owl?" Sherry whispered.

Jimmy cupped his hands and imitated the notes. He repeated the call. The hooting came back more rapidly this time.

Jimmy grabbed the penlight and said to Sherry, "Let's go see!"

They scrambled out of the hole and, side by side on hands and knees, peered through the lightly falling snow into the dark woods beyond. The vague silhouettes of tree trunks looked like spirits from a dream world. Jimmy directed the weak beam of light from right to left.

"Go back there!" Sherry pointed.

Standing between two snow towers was a gray workhorse. Sitting on it was Hawk. He wore a wide brimmed hat powdered with snow. His long, gray hair flowed from under the hat over the shoulders of his deer hide coat.

"Hey ho," he called out, "you two pilgrims got any hot coffee for a weary traveler?"

"Hawk!" Jimmy shouted. "It's Hawk!"

They both stood up and sank deep into the snow. Hawk nudged the horse that waded over to them. "Looks like right comfortable lodgings," he said. "Where are your snowshoes?"

"They're inside, Hawk. Boy, are we ever glad to see you. How'd you find us?"

"Old Star here did the work. She knows these hills better'n me. You're only a little bit off the trail. All I did was keep calling. Down the hill a ways I almost got knocked off the horse by an owl. I musta said something he didn't like. By the way, who's this?" he said nodding toward Sherry.

"Oh, Hawk, this is Sherry. Sherry, Hawk."

"Hi, Mr. Hawk. Jimmy's been talking about you all day."

"Just call me Hawk, no mister with that. He's got some imagination that Jimmy does. Best to divide everything he says by two to get at the part that's true unless, of course, he was saying good things."

Jimmy slid back into their cave and emerged with the blanket, their packs and the snowshoes. Hawk had already unsaddled Old Star. He removed the red and yellow striped blanket and handed it to Sherry. "Old Star's been keepin' this warm for you. Wrap up in it and we'll be going."

Hawk took the wool blanket from Jimmy, threw it over the horses back and cinched the saddle down. Old Star whinnied, stomped his great hooves and blew puffs of air from his nostrils. "Being a special guest of Jimmy's," Hawk said to Sherry, "you get to ride." He lifted her in one easy motion up into the saddle. "Now don't you worry none about Old Star. She's a kindly old lady."

Sherry said, "Hawk, is my father really mad at me and Jimmy?"

"Not by a long shot. He and Joe never made it back either. They called Martha from the bar at the Colonial Hotel in Smethport. All the roads are closed down tight. Martha told him some men were out looking for you two, but he shouldn't worry."

"There are others looking for us?" Jimmy asked.

"About a dozen on snowmobiles led by Lewis. He and his buddies were all down at the beer garden when your mother called. I imagine most of 'em have hit trees or drove into ravines by now. Especially Big Charlie, Sr.! He's got a boy in your class who told him about the wolves. Got a gun rack on his snowmobile." He looked at Jimmy whose face had gone slack. "Not to worry, though. That whole family's none too bright. Probably he's accidentally shot himself along the logging road. Damn fools, the lot of 'em!. Whoever finds you is supposed to fire a couple of shots to call off the search. But I'm old. Most likely I'll forget to do that by the time we get back. Maybe I'll shoot a couple of arrows instead. Serve 'em right. We better get a move on. It's well after midnight."

"Really?" said Sherry. "We thought it was early."

"Let me have a pair of those snowshoes, Jimmy. I'll lead, you follow." Hawk tied a rope to the saddlehorn and handed the loops to Jimmy. "Keep a hold of this. We don't want you wandering off again."

"Did Pa and Mr. Woolman get that bear they were after?" Jimmy asked.

"No, but Woolman got off one shot with the dart gun. Missed the bear, but tranquilized a squirrel to death. Too much juice for such a little critter. Your ma said Joe told him to get it mounted. A kind of trophy." Hawk turned to Sherry. "Your dad will be too busy living that down to be upset with you. You warm enough up there?"

"Yes, I am. Thanks," she said pulling the blanket tightly around her neck.

"Did you get the shakes earlier?"

"Yes, I couldn't stop shivering."

"Jimmy here tell you the cure?"

"He said we needed to be close together to share our body heat."

"That's a good one, Jimmy. I'll have to remember it next time I'm lost in a storm with a pretty girl." Hawk smiled. Sherry gave Jimmy a look.

"But, Hawk," Jimmy protested, "you told me . . ."

"Best we be going," said Hawk. He removed a three-foot stick from his shoulder sack and handed it to Jimmy. "Hold this a minute." He got a small box of wooden matches from his pocket and struck one, which he held to the rags, wrapped around one end. They burst into flame. He took the torch from Jimmy and handed it to Sherry. "Think you can hold this and still ride?"

"I think so," she said.

"It'll burn long enough to get us out of the woods. Be careful of your hair and try not to set the horse on fire," Hawk grinned.

Hawk took Old Star's reins and moved forward. They plodded slowly through a corridor of pines, up the side of a ravine into a patch of laurel buried in snow. The bushes looked like the humped backs of sleeping bears. The yellow light of the torch danced on the snow, among the branches and on the travelers. Often Sherry looked back at Jimmy to make sure he was still there. The snowfall had abated, visibility improved.

As they entered the last stand of hardwoods between them and home, Jimmy shouted to Hawk, "Hey, Hawk!"

"What?"

"Sherry saw Romeo and Juliet."

"I know," he called back.

"How could you know?"

"I saw it in her eyes. Unlike the tongue, eyes never lie."

19

So, Jimmy, Mr. Fletcher asked us to exchange journals, have a partner read a few pages and then be a guest writer for one entry. I feel a bit nervous writing in your beautiful journal. It would be better if we could just write notes to each other, ones the teacher wouldn't read. After all, that's a form of writing, too. I wonder why no English teacher has ever made notes an assignment. They'd just be asking us to do what we do anyway. At least we'd be writing, and we could certainly be more honest.

Honestly, though, you know I've already read all of your journal. From it I learned so much. I had no idea that wolves were so social, so dedicated to one another within their pack. They really take care of each other like family. They live together and hunt together. What's really neat, I think, is that each of the adults in the pack helps raise the pups. The aunts, uncles and cousins all pitch in to help the parents get food, teach the pups, play with them and protect them. One even stays behind to baby-sit while the other adults hunt. That's so cool!

The other things I liked in your journal were the stories. Most of them came from your friend Hawk. He must be a very good friend to tell you things like how the stars came to be, about his visit to the stone medicine wheel out west and that wonderful story, the *Going Away Tale*, about the wolf named Shadow. So moving.

One of the things I'm going to begin doing in my own journal is using the internet to get stories about fly fishing trips. The people you quoted wrote first hand accounts of seeing wolf pups and adults interacting with each other and with other animals like bears and buffalo. Very powerful writing!

Jimmy, I've saved the best for last. What an imagination you have! I love your ongoing story of Romeo and Juliet, your two fictional wolves. I certainly remember the play. The descriptions in each of your encounters were so clear, so vivid that I felt as though I was right there with you. Each word drew me more and more into the scenes. As you explained the smoke ceremony, I performed it in my head. I could smell the pine scent and see the snow falling. As you waited, almost in a trance like state, I waited, too. When you looked through the smoke and saw the wolves standing side by side, I saw them as well. They were beautiful, the black wolf and the white wolf.

Thank you for letting me hike with you through the deep snows of your imagination. I could even feel how cold it must have been. Even so, I'm ready to go again. I can't wait for you to write more entries. Please let me read them. I'd love to tag along on more of your adventures.

18 March: Guest Writer in Fly Fishing Journal, Jimmy Warren

Dear Sherry,

I like the idea of being able to write in your journal and that you are writing in mine. You're a good writer. Sometimes I don't always know what you're talking about when you use specific fly fishing terms that relate to tying flies or when you name the flies you use. But that just means I have more to learn. So I guess you could say that you are my teacher.

While many of your entries show the beauty and grace of fly fishing, none does it better than the one where you described the 'perfect day' you had on Willowemoc Creek in the Catskill Mountains up in New York State. I could feel the energy of that day come right through your writing.

You were fishing upstream from your parents about a half mile. So you were alone. There was a shack back in the woods on the far bank. The only sign of life was the wood smoke coming from the stovepipe chimney. I could hear the water rushing by; hear it muttering where rocks were partially exposed.

What I got from that entry was that you weren't just fishing. You had become part of the landscape, part of the steep mountains that rose up from the stream bed, part of the sky where puffed clouds floated, white on blue, part of the wind that carried the scent of skunk cabbage and the earthworm fragrance of water that has run off the mountains from spring snowmelt, part of the moving stream where you waved your line through the air to rest above pools that boiled green with eddies.

You said in that entry that you felt disconnected from the rest of the world, that yesterday evaporated and tomorrow did not exist. It was just you in that moment along with the bald eagle fishing further upstream, and later, in the early afternoon, the black bear that crossed the creek without realizing you were there. Few people I've met have ever achieved that level of peace. Generally, they are so wound up in their lives that they aren't able to let go. After reading your journal, I think that that is exactly why you fish. It's a way to let go. It's the same reason I love to be in the woods tracking, to lose track of myself. Probably what you do, Sherry, and what I do are both some form of natural meditation, a way to get away from worries, regrets, schoolwork, and people who exasperate us. It is also a way to get closer to who we really are, to understand our own dreams and have the time to dream them.

How else can you explain the 'perfect day' fly fishing when you didn't even catch any fish. I think you caught something more important. Thanks for switching journals with me. I hope, too, that you'll keep being my teacher. I'd love to learn how to fish for eagles, bears, clouds and mountains.

20

From his upstairs bedroom, Jimmy heard the knock at the front door. He had been daydreaming about Sherry and hadn't heard anyone drive up. It had been over a month since they had been stranded in the storm yet he loved recalling every detail of their time together. It was a new story he kept telling to himself. It was a real story, not fiction like his old fantasies about her. It seemed to him like a story he would make up, invent, throw in all the specific details so that he could hold on to it in his mind, but it wasn't that way at all. The fire, the wolves, the kiss, the cave tree were seared to his memory like a brand. It was this reverie that the knock at the door had interrupted.

Downstairs chairs shuffled and his mother called out, "Just a minute!" Then there were muffled voices and feet stomping snow from boots. Jimmy looked out his window. Parked down by the barn were the sheriff's squad car and an old pickup with more rust than red paint. Even though it was dusk, he could see two rifles with scopes in the truck's gun rack.

Joe yelled up to him, "Jimmy, you've got company! Come on down, son!"

Three men were seated on the flowered living room sofa when

Jimmy entered. The sheriff was sitting in the easy chair. Martha sat in the Morris chair by the woodstove, and Joe stood next to her. Mounted on the wall behind them was the head of an eight-point buck, the same one whose tanned skin had become the cover to Jimmy's journal. His glassy eyes watched. Leaning in the corner was the carved walking stick, a story in wood, which held the truth that the uninvited guests had come for.

"Jimmy," Joe said, "these guys asked if they could have a word with you. It has something to do with wolves."

Instantly Jimmy felt sick. His legs were rubber. He wanted to run; his stomach was about to heave. Instead he sunk like dead weight into the captain's chair. "Yes, what?" he whispered.

Joe continued, "You already know Sheriff Lyle. This here is Grimes, his deputy." Both men wore gray uniforms with a black stripe up the side of each pant leg, had square handled pistols secured in black holsters with leather flaps and held their coats in their laps. Sheriff Lyle had thin hair the color of his uniform and a smile fixed on his square face. Grimes, much younger, had a badge on his shirt, wore a wide brimmed, gray hat and looked very serious.

Joe went on, "These two are Charlie and Ed Tanner. It seems Charlie has a son in your class. He's the one you told me about."

"Ah, well, yes. Big Charlie," Jimmy spoke hesitantly looking at the two men. Ed was thin and nervous. He had a dingy blue coat on. His denim coveralls were several sizes to big for his slight frame and raised up at the ankles exposing red long underwear that disappeared into black rubber boots. His smile revealed a few yellowish teeth. The rest were missing. He nodded continuously as his eyes darted from person to person. Ed kept shifting his weight and didn't seem to quite know what to do with his hands.

Charlie had a broad grin on his broad face. He was the size of two men. He wore an immense snowmobile suit that showed considerable wear and had greasy stretch marks where his ample belly pushed against the zippered fabric.

"You do know my boy, then," Charlie was the first to speak. "You two had a kinda situation at that school."

Jimmy said quickly, "Oh, I'm so sorry about that, Mr. Tanner. Charlie just didn't give me a choice. He just wouldn't let up, kept teasing me about dead wolves and then he tackled me in the cafeteria. I told my parents about it. I even apologized to the teacher who broke it up. It was our English teacher. You can ask him about it; he saw the whole thing."

"Not here 'bout that," Charlie said, his voice a rasp chewing the edge off a plank. "The boy's an idiot at home. Don't spect he'd be any different at school. Besides, he got that black eye to think on fer a while. Principal gave me a call, too. He explained it all and said to keep him home for a few days. Charlie's cleanin' out the chicken coop right now wishin' he were back at school. No worse chore on the planet.

"I did talk to that English teacher of yers. Fletcher. I asked him to show me that journal, the wolf one. But he said he didn't have it and wouldn't give it me even if he did. So we come right to the source which is you, boy."

Jimmy shoved his hands in his pockets to keep from trembling. Martha opened the flue damper and the door to the woodstove. She slid in a split piece of shagbark hickory. The wood began to snap and spit in the flames. She closed the door and sat back in her chair watching Jimmy.

"According to my boy, he overheard Fletcher talking to some teachers, and he said them wolves you write about was real. We'd like to take a look see in yer book and judge fer ourselves. You have any objections, boy?"

"I have an objection," Joe said. "First of all, I don't like the tone of your voice. He isn't 'boy,' he's Jimmy. Use his name when you speak to him. Secondly, that journal is Jimmy's private writing and no one has a right to read it without his permission. Which of the two of you can read, anyway?"

"We brought Grimes for that," Charlie said.

Joe said, "You can't get a warrant because he hasn't broken the law. Isn't that right, Lyle?"

"Now, Joe, no reason to get all riled up here. My job is to protect the public. If there are wolves about, the people have a right to know.

We're just lookin' for information, trying to track down a story that's been circulating in town, that's all. You're boy hasn't done a thing wrong; you're right about that. We're just askin'. It all seems preposterous to me and Grimes here, but if Jimmy knows something, he should tell us."

Joe moved next to Jimmy and said, "Let's just say, for the sake of argument, there really are wolves up in these hills. Who would protect them?"

"If there's wolves up there," Charlie said shifting his great weight and massaging the white stubble on one of his chins, "they's dead! I'll see ta that! Can't have no goddamn wolves runnin' loose 'round here! They's sure enough varmints, killin' machines; cows, goats, horses, chickens, don't matter to them. Only a crazy person wouldn't shoot 'em on sight!"

"Ya, shshshshoot 'em, ya!" Ed blurted out.

"You kin know the source for my suspicion," Charlie continued. "A month back when we was looking for yer boy and the Woolman girl up Two Mile, I heard howling and it weren't the wind and it wasn't no coyote neither. What say to that, Jimmy boy?"

Jimmy started to answer not knowing what he was going to say, but his father spoke first. "Charlie, you're just hearing what you want to hear. The wind that night was like the howling of a hundred wolves, moans and cries coming from every tree. If I remember correctly, Lewis told me you all had been down at the bar for quite a while before you went on the rescue. And as for your son overhearing Fletcher, he probably thought realistic meant real. Writing a story and being real are two very different things. And even if the wolves were real, you, Charlie Tanner, would be committing a federal offense, a violation of the Endangered Species Act, if you harmed them in any way. That means jail time, Charlie! I suggest all of you go pay Woolman a visit. He's the law when it comes to wild animals. He'll tell you the same thing."

Charlie did not hesitate, "Woolman's a fool, a first class idiot! I ain't about to visit with someone's been trying to lock me up for poachin'.

Wouldn't believe a word he said. I'm warnin' ya, Jimmy boy, if they're up there, I'll find 'em and nail their hides to the wall of my shed!"

Jimmy took a long breath to compose himself. He looked directly at Charlie whose dark eyes he had been avoiding. "The problem, Mr. Tanner, with hunting fictional wolves is that there is nothing to shoot at. They only exist up here." He pointed to his head.

The front door swung open and in walked Hawk. "What's wrong?" he said stomping his boots on the hall rug. "Someone get hurt?"

"We were just leavin'," Lyle got up. The other three stood as well. "Sorry we bothered you folks. Just trying to track down the truth is all. We won't be botherin' you any longer."

Charlie faced Hawk. "What you know 'bout them wolves up Two Mile?"

Hawk smiled. "You been drinkin', Charlie? This here is Pennsylvania! Only wolf 'round here is over at the courthouse in Smethport. Go take a look. You could probably shoot him. Or you might try up in Canada somewheres. I hear there are still a few up there, old ones though, with bad teeth." He looked straight at Ed who flinched.

"Let's be on our way, Charlie," Lyle herded the three men toward the door. "We've bothered these good people enough. Sorry, Joe, Martha. Goodbye, Jimmy, Hawk."

Once the door had closed behind the men, Hawk said, "Looks like you had a little drama here. Sorry I missed it. What happened?"

"Tanner brought Lyle here to find out about Jimmy's wolves," Martha said. "Tanner is an awful man. I don't like to speak ill of people, he really gives me the creeps. Ignorance is a frightening thing. We better have a set down and talk this out. I'll make some coffee."

Joe patted his son on the back. "Doesn't look good, Jimmy. I don't think they believed us. All of Charlie's talk about livestock was real bull. He ain't got but a few chickens. Hardly a meal for a wolf. He and that brother of his is just trigger happy, always have been."

In the kitchen Jimmy sat at the round oak table covering his face with his hands continuously taking deep breaths. Hawk sensed that he was near tears. Martha put coffee out for everyone, uncovered the sugar bowl and placed a bottle of milk on the table.

"I guess we couldn't expect to keep the wolves a secret for ever," Joe said. "We knew this was comin'. You can bet Tanner and his skinny brother are going to be up there taking a good look around as soon as the snow's out which will be in a week. Even though we don't like it, they are good at one thing; they can track. The both of 'em are wildlife bounty hunters even though bounty's been off everything for quite some time. It's like no one told them."

Hawk stirred his coffee with a spoon and put his other hand on Jimmy's arm. "I'm not sure it's all that bad, Jimmy," he said. "Romeo and Juliet didn't get here by being dumb. They made it all this way by being inconspicuous, staying out of sight, avoiding detection. Wolves are like that, secretive. I think they accepted you, Jimmy, as part of their territory. To them you're a creature of like spirit. If you weren't, believe me, you never would have seen them, you'd have only seen tracks.

"Well, there are true stories going back hundreds of years about wolves who couldn't be caught. One in New Mexico, a lobo, had fifty wolfers after it 'cause the bounty was so high. They put out calf meat laced with strychnine, set steel traps soaked in wolf urine, set snares, rode the hills on mules carrying special long distance rifles to shoot that wolf. They got nothing for their efforts. They'd stay in the wild for weeks at a time. Nothin'. Even hunt all night. Nothin'. Just tracks. That wolf knew his territory, must've had a picture of it in his head. Only fed on his own fresh kills. His tracks always led to rocks where they just disappeared. Some of the wolfers even came to believe that this wolf had the power to change into something else.

"One by one, the wolfers dropped out. Even the top wolfer from Canada had met his match. There was some talk that the wolf was hid by the tribes during the day, but I'm not sure about the truth of that. Our people sometimes like to take credit for situations that involve courage and intelligence. It gives them a sense of power. They like to think that they have the same qualities as that lobo wolf and can survive no matter who is trying to hunt them down. Come to think of it, some of them did have those qualities or else I wouldn't be here.

"But the point is," Hawk continued after sipping his coffee, "your wolves have those qualities. I don't think Charlie and his half-wit brother are a match for Romeo and Juliet. They may find tracks, they may set traps or even ride Two Mile on horseback, but it will always be as though those wolves have evaporated."

"I think Hawk is right, Jimmy," Martha tried to reassure her son. "Your wolves aren't deer who stand out in a field waiting to get shot. They aren't reckless like wild dogs. They're smart, Jimmy. They're careful. I think they'll both be okay."

Joe set down his coffee cup. "Ya know, Jimmy, if the Tanners do go up there looking around and tramp all over the place, the wolves may just move on. They could head south of here where there's still a lot of wild country up on the Allegheny plateau. Or they might just head back home, wherever that is, Canada or the Adirondacks up in New York. I wouldn't worry so much. Too bad though, there isn't some way you could warn Romeo and Juliet just to give them a head start, let them know that those jerks are on their way."

Hawk said, "Mind if I help myself to another cup, Martha? Sure is good coffee."

"Go right ahead," she said.

The coffee steamed in Hawk's cup as he continued, "There may be a way to warn 'em. We could go up there come Saturday and raise some hell. Try to scare 'em off ourselves. Shoot off guns, throw sticks, rocks, snowballs, anything to let 'em know they're not welcome anymore. It means, Jimmy, breaking our trust with 'em. They won't understand, but it just might save their lives. The snow's gone soft so we can get back in there on horses."

Jimmy looked at his parents and Hawk. His eyes were wet. "I'd be willing to do that," he said. "I won't like it, but I'll do it. If that doesn't work, I hope you guys are right about all that other stuff. I have a bad feeling about this. My hands are still shaking and my palms are all sweaty."

"It'll be okay, son," Joe said. "Loving anything, woman, home or wolf, is a risk worth taking."

"So, Jimmy," Hawk said, "speaking of love, why don't you ask your woman to come along on Saturday?"

"My woman?" Jimmy said.

"Yes, you know, your girlfriend. She's a tough one, not delicate like most of your town girls. By the way, have you gotten around to asking her old man how many horses he wants for that daughter of his?"

Jimmy smiled and wiped his eyes. "I don't think it's done that way anymore, Hawk."

"Well, I guess I've been out of the loop for some time. You mean to tell me if I find a handsome woman who'll have me, I don't have to trade Old Star for her?"

Martha said, "You might have to trade some blankets, but you'll be able to keep that horse."

"I'm just teasing the boy, Martha."

"Jimmy," said Joe, "why not give Sherry a call and see if she's free Saturday. You'll need all the help you can get."

"I will as soon as the kitchen clears out. I don't like an audience when I'm talking to her."

Joe turned to Hawk, "Let's finish our coffee in by the woodstove."

"But I want to listen," said Hawk. "How else will I learn to sweet talk the girls? Jimmy could probably teach me a few things."

"Come along. Give Jimmy some space," Joe said pushing his chair back.

"I'll just look in on the girls," Martha said. "They should be asleep by now if they haven't set up listening to us."

Jimmy whispered on the phone. He explained to Sherry everything that had gone on that evening. He told Hawk's wolf story and repeated what his parents had said. Then he asked if she would be able to help out on Saturday.

"I'll be there, Jimmy," she said so faintly. He knew that she was already crying. "What should I tell my father? He doesn't know that Romeo and Juliet are real. Should I tell him?" Her sentences came out amidst gulps of air and loud sniffling.

"Sherry, everything's going to be all right. Just tell your dad that

Hawk is taking us horseback riding up the logging road. That's all he needs to know."

"Maybe he could help, Jimmy, if we told him the truth. He could tranquilize them and take them to a more remote place. He does it all the time with bears."

"Let's try to drive them away ourselves first. If that doesn't work, I'll tell him the truth; I'll tell everyone the truth."

"Okay, Jimmy. I hope Hawk is right, but I'm scared. Will you still come over Friday night like we planned?"

"Sure, I wouldn't miss dinner with the folks. Are they going to ask me a lot of awkward questions?"

"Oh, no. It'll be nice. You know they both like you. Mom will ask how your mom is doing and about school. Dad will tell a lot of silly jokes. You just have to remember to laugh at the right times. Then we'll play Scrabble. Try not to win, though. Mom likes to win. Dad said he could give you a ride home around eleven or so, if that's okay with your parents?"

"It's fine with them. They like you, too. So, I guess I'll see you at school tomorrow."

"Jimmy," Sherry lowered her voice so that it was barely audible, "don't worry about Romeo and Juliet. It'll all work out, really. I miss them already, and I'm not nearly as close to them as you. I just want you to know that I miss you, too, and, and that, well, I want you to know that I love you, Jimmy. Is it okay to say that?"

"It is," Jimmy smiled. "I feel the same way about you. I'll see you tomorrow, then?"

"Yes, tomorrow," Sherry whispered.

21

wj 5 April

The original range of the gray wolf stretched from northern Maine to the Olympic Peninsula in the state of Washington. Two smaller subspecies, the red wolf, populated the south, and the Mexican wolf, the southwest into Mexico. In the American wilderness, before the coming of the white man, the wolf reigned supreme feeding on elk, moose, buffalo, pronghorn antelope, mountain goats and bighorn sheep, mule deer and whitetails, as well as a plethora (see thesaurus) of smaller mammals such as marmots and pikas.

For the first several hundred years after they arrived, settlers carried on a campaign to exterminate the wolf. Except for northern Minnesota, they were successful. Poison meat was left on trails for the wolves to consume. They were caught in steel tooth traps and in snares. If they were still alive when found, they were shot or clubbed to death. Some pioneer journals retell incidents where female wolves were followed back to their dens where, while the mother was inside feeding her pups, the den was dynamited.

There are early photographs that exist which show bounty hunters posing in front of their light planes. Lined up on the ground and hanging from the wings of the plane are the ragged carcasses of wolves.

My mother says that ignorance is a frightening thing. It was ignorance and fear, as I have said before, that killed the wolf. I have always thought that as a species, man was still evolving. Now, I'm not sure. There are still many people who lack an understanding of the importance of wolves, of other animals, birds, insects and plants. They see the natural world as serving them. If it doesn't satisfy their needs directly or if it's in the way, shoot it, cut it down, throw it away. It has no right to exist.

When I conjure up Romeo and Juliet in my imagined wilderness, I only have to make eye contact to know they have as much right to live in the world as you, Mr. Fletcher, and me. Probably someone has already said it, but the truth is man cannot live without nature; however, nature can certainly live without him. That's something to think about. We need a planet that is healthy, in balance, complete. If we spoil the air, the water, the land and all those things that live on it, we spoil our own lives. We are less because the wolf is gone.

There are people today who do understand and so there is hope. They are the ones who brought the wolf back to Wyoming, who are reintroducing it to Montana, Idaho, Arizona and the south. They are studying the east for possible wolf release sites. They are also the people in Minnesota, in Canada and Alaska who, upon seeing a wolf in the wild, do not pull the trigger, who are not afraid, but who marvel at its beauty and count the sighting as one of the finest moments of their lives.

We live in a fast-paced, information age, one where I can, from our little farm up Lillibridge Creek, talk on line with people from all over the world. I wonder, though, if we are seeking the right information, and I wonder if we aren't moving so fast that we run the risk of running over ourselves.

As for me, I want to live in a world that is a little more deliberate, a little less superficial and self-centered. Give me an earth where Romeo and Juliet roam free in their forest where one day I might pass through and glimpse their grace in hopes that some of it will rub off on me.

Forgive me, Mr. Fletcher, for rambling on so. I've just been worried lately. Every night's been filled with ominous dreams that haunt me during the day. One, in particular, really scared me. I was caught in a steel trap. My ankle bled as I tried to wriggle out. Then I heard horse hooves pounding through the dark woods toward me. I struggled to get free, but couldn't. The horses stopped in the night shadows. Then two grizzly looking men approached me. They were laughing and pointing. The shot woke me up.

I thought if I got it all out in my journal, I'd feel better. You know, Mr. Fletcher, the 'therapeutic value' of writing you've talked to us about. Sometimes that really does work. Unfortunately, it didn't this time.

22

Woolman's green truck moved along the Lillibridge Creek Road, its headlights feeling the macadam like a pair of silver antennae. The midnight darkness was punctuated with the iridescent eyes of deer feeding in pastures. Sherry and Jimmy were watching for any that may be in the road or about to cross it.

"There's one, daddy!" Sherry said squeezing Jimmy's hand, which they were both doing, in turn, with each sighting.

"Maybe we need a spring hunting season this year. Winter didn't thin the herd out much," Woolman said slowing as he passed a group of five whitetails that were bumping into each other trying to jump back over the barbed wire fence. "Jimmy, you'll be driving soon. You need to remember when you see a deer crossing the road, he's not the one you need to worry about. It's the one following him that you don't see who can be real trouble. There's a nurse up at Cole in Coudersport who works the night shift. Her husband told her never to swerve off the highway if a deer runs in front of her, which is good advice. You're less likely to get injured hitting a deer than a tree. In two weeks she hit five deer giving them enough venison for several families. Her car was a mess, though. Then her husband told her that he forgot to say that it would be okay if she used her brakes."

Jimmy smiled and said, "You know Lewis who works at the farm. He says that when the men are talking about the best rifle for deer, a Remington 30-30, a 30-40 Craig or a 30-06, he says he prefers his Ford truck. He's been driving all winter with just one headlight."

They were quiet for a while watching dimly lit farmhouses pass. The only light at Old Man Swanson's was a lantern glowing in the barn. The Nelson place was dark. Above the black shoulders of the mountains that bordered the valley were the sparks of stars that looked to Jimmy like distant campfires.

The road rose, curved around a hillside and leveled out for the final straight stretch before Jimmy's farm would come into view. The warm spring air that blew in the partially opened windows smelled of earthworms, mud and manure, a fragrance that would in years to come trigger in Jimmy all the memories of these beautiful and terrible days.

"I want to thank you, Mr. Woolman, for such a nice night. You and Mrs. Woolman made me feel very comfortable. I even enjoyed the Scrabble," Jimmy said squeezing Sherry's hand again.

"I'm glad you had a good time. We wanted you to know that we weren't mad at you for getting stuck in that snowstorm with our daughter. In fact, we were grateful that you took such good care of her. Also, I could have listened to your wolf tales all night. Hope my stories weren't too boring."

"Not at all. They were great. That one about the tranquilized bear waking up in the back seat of the station wagon was so funny. I would have loved to see the expression on your face when you looked in the rear view mirror." Jimmy pointed up ahead. "Oh, my turn off is right up here. There's the house right . . ." His voice trailed off. "I wonder what's wrong," he said puzzled. "Every light in the house is on. My folks never do that, especially this late."

The plank bridge rattled like low thunder as the truck crossed and eased to a stop in the dooryard. Jimmy opened the door and slid out. Sherry got out as well.

"I'll be right back, daddy. I just want to make sure Jimmy makes it to the door safely." She gave her dad a sly smile.

"Good night, Jimmy," Woolman said turning off the headlights.

"Good night, Mr. Woolman. Thanks again."

Sherry took Jimmy's hand and they walked into the yellow light of the front porch.

"I wonder what's going on."

"Maybe they're just waiting up for you, Jimmy."

"I doubt it."

The front door opened and Lewis stepped out onto the front porch. He wore brown coveralls, a red and black plaid shirt and still had on his black rubber, barn boots. Jimmy knew his mother never let anyone in the house with boots.

"Hey, Lewis, what's wrong?"

"Wrong? Why nothin' I can think of," he smiled behind a weeks worth of gray whiskers. "I come out to say hello to Miss Woolman and her old man. I'll just go on out and wish him a good night."

Lewis walked down the steps and crossed the yard to the truck. The two men talked in whispers.

Sherry turned to Jimmy, put her arms around his neck and kissed him for a long moment until Jimmy broke free and gasped, "Sherry, not right in front of your dad!"

"Jimmy, he knows we aren't just friends. Besides it's good for him to get used to the fact that he's not the only man in my life now. Dads always have trouble with that. You're in my life now, and I want the whole world to know. Jimmy, you're blushing."

"That's what I do when I'm happy. And I couldn't be happier than I am right now. I really do love you, Sherry."

Jimmy leaned forward and kissed her. He whispered, "My dad and I will be over to pick you up around nine or so. Hawk says he doesn't like to wake the horses up too early. We'll try to convince those wolves to move on to a safer territory."

"It'll be okay. I'll be ready. Sweet dreams, Jimmy, sweet dreams."

As Sherry walked back to the truck, Lewis handed Woolman a small manila envelope, shook his hand and walked to where Jimmy stood. The two lingered at the edge of the pool of porch light watching the red taillights recede up the drive until well after the rumble of the bridge died away across the dark fields.

Jimmy turned when he heard the house door open. His mother and father stood by the railing. Martha said, "You boys come in now. It's very late." Her voice had a quiver in it, so slight, a half breath instead of a full one. Few would have noticed, but Jimmy was well schooled in the world of details. He noticed.

"Ma, dad, will you tell me what the problem is? Are the girls okay? Did the wild dogs get in the barn? Why are all the lights on? Where's Hawk?"

Joe said, "We've been waiting for you, son. The girls are fine, asleep up stairs. No dogs either. Hawk's fine, too. You're right, though, there is trouble. But we need to sit down in the living room and talk out how it happened and what we can do about it. Lewis, you come in, too."

"Come on, Jimmy," said Martha. It was when his parents turned and the full light of the porch illuminated their faces that Jimmy could see the serious look in his father's eyes and that his mother had been crying.

Jimmy and his mother sat on the sofa, Lewis in the Morris chair by the opened woodstove and Joe stood leaning against the entryway, his arms crossed.

"Jimmy," Joe began, his voice wavering, searching for words, "parents really try to protect their kids from having to deal with hard situations. God knows there's plenty of that to deal with once you've grown. But sometimes things happen that we can't control. This is one of those times. If it was an accident we had to deal with, it would be easier to accept than what has happened. What was done was done on purpose and it has to do with your wolves." Joe looked at Lewis. "Lewis, tell Jimmy what happened tonight the way you told it to us."

Jimmy felt the stone of dread forming in his chest. He instinctively knew what Lewis was going to say and felt helpless against the words he did not want to hear. He had no power to stop them, hold them at bay. If only he could run, could cover his ears. He looked at Lewis.

"Now, Jimmy, this ain't easy fer me. I was down at the taproom having a few sips when the Tanner brothers burst in whoopin' and hollerin' and carryin' on. The gist of their bragging was that they shot two wolves about a quarter mile from the Rocks, a black and a white. Seems they tracked them from near the head of Two Mile Creek down along the ridge, set up traps, caught the black right around sunup, shot him and used him for bait to trap the white knowing that she wouldn't leave her mate. That black wolf musta walked into the traps as innocent as a child."

Jimmy's heart clenched. He went numb and could barely hear the rest of the story. Lewis sounded far away as if maybe this was another nightmare, a bad dream.

"By sundown they caught the white in a steel trap. She had nearly gnawed through her leg to get loose, but they showed up and shot her, too. Those Tanners are ignorant, low life sons-a-bitches. They think it takes a real man to do what they done. What it takes is a damn fool. They strung up the carcasses from a tree in the Square across from the bar. I had my old camera in the truck and convinced them to let me take their pictures next to the dead wolves. When Woolman drove up tonight, I gave him an envelope with the film and a list of a dozen witnesses who'll be glad to testify in court as to who killed the wolves. Some of 'em may be drunks, but they's honest people. I asked Woolman not to interfere 'til mornin' to give us a chance to bring the wolves back here.

"After I took the picture of them boys, we went back to the bar. I bought Charlie and his idiot brother Ed a beer, and then promptly knocked the both of 'em on their ass, pardon the language, Martha. I did that to save you the effort, Jimmy, knowin' how hurt you'd be by this. You don't have to worry about them two. Woolman will pick 'em up in the mornin'. He was worried about us buryin' the evidence out here, but then thought the photographs and witnesses would do just fine. I gotta tell ya, Jimmy, it breaks my heart to bring home news like this."

Joe said, "We knew something like this might happen. Hawk's waiting in town to make sure no one takes them. He thought you'd like to bring them back here and bury them down by the creek. Is he right about that? Jimmy, you want to go with us to get Romeo and Juliet?"

Jimmy couldn't get any words to come out. He stared at the glowing coals in the woodstove. Deer eyes, he thought, stars, yellow wolf eyes. And the tears came silently, the dam that holds back the lake of emotion burst. He covered his face with his hands and sobbed while visions formed of woodsmoke rising, falling snow and the calm wolves who watched him, who pressed each other, licked muzzles and rubbed heads. He heard their howls, saw their erect ears filtering subtle sounds, sniffed the air with them as they read the wind.

Romeo and Juliet were dead. He had so hoped that this would be a different play than the one he had read in school. His father was right. He must bring them back to the farm; bury them within the sound of running water.

Finally, Jimmy raised his head. "I'll go," he said.

"Why don't we take my truck, Joe," said Lewis. "It has a muffler. It'll be a lot quieter than the farm truck."

"True enough. We don't want to attract any attention."

The phone rang and Martha went to answer it. Jimmy, his father and Lewis prepared to leave. Martha returned and said, "That was Hawk. He said it's getting near closing time at the bar so you better hurry."

It was quiet in the truck as Lewis drove the creek road toward town. The single headlight penetrated thin fog as if it were a lighthouse beam searching the dark. Jimmy was aware that the air had cooled; he smelled the gasoline odor of the old truck and recorded in his memory every creaking sound mixed with the drone of the engine. Even though all of his senses were on high alert, he stared straight ahead, his face a shadowy yellow illuminated by the dashboard lights. In his head he knew that he would remember this ride and the awful truth he carried with him now just an hour after having followed this same dark road with Sherry feeling, in his love for her, indestructible. No greater happiness had he known. Now, no greater sorrow.

Lewis followed Mill Street down the sloping hill into town. Dense fog had rolled in from the Allegheny River muting each streetlight along Main and Pearl. Lewis stopped at the light even though it was green. The town was deserted. Jimmy's eyes tried to peel away the mist in order to see the trees in the Square, but it was useless. He could only make out the silhouette of the large stone that held the engraved names of the town's war dead, the chrome base of the flagpole and some of the bare maples, which lined the walk.

"There!" said Joe. "Hawk flashed his lights. He's by the firehouse."

Lewis drove slowly down Main Street past the closed theater, the spiraling sign of the barber shop, the long row of old, red brick buildings that housed the dark laundromat, the shoe shop, the hardware.

Hawk was standing beside his truck when Lewis pulled up. Joe got out, talked with him and returned to the truck.

"Jimmy, why don't you and me ride in the back. Lewis, follow Hawk. He said you should back in. And turn off your lights. The Tanners are still in the bar."

Lewis backed over the curb and along the stakes and rope that had marked the perimeter of the ice skating rink that now held a few inches of water and mud.

Jimmy's heart was racing. He thought that if this were a dream, now would be the time to wake up. Beyond was the dull red beer sign that hung in the tavern window. The truck moved slowly through the misty dark passing barren trees whose branches reached out like the bony arms of ghosts. Then Jimmy saw them, the dark shadows of their bodies hanging head down, forelegs stretched out as if they were in full stride.

As the truck moved closer, Jimmy could see the black and white of their fur, and, closer still, the red stain of dried blood that ran the length of their throats and gathered in a dark pool on the ground below. Their hind legs were bound with ropes tied to a tree branch.

At first he felt paralyzed by the sight. Lewis backed the bed of the truck under the two wolves. Hawk touched Jimmy's shoulder, handed him a hunting knife and said, "Jimmy, you cut them down. Joe and I will lower them into the truck."

Jimmy stood and sliced the ropes one at a time. Joe and Hawk cradled each body and laid them head forward in the bed. Jimmy cut the ropes free from each of their hind legs and sat leaning against the cab. "Let's go," he said.

Joe turned to Hawk, "Tanners'll be after us as soon as they find out the wolves are gone."

Hawk held up a distributor cap and a hand full of tangled wires. "Not unless they carry extra parts." He smiled.

"I have a feeling you've done this before."

"No, I just read about it someplace."

Lewis said, "You can read?"

"I can read your fortune if you don't get moving. Jimmy, you want me to ride back here with you?"

"No, Hawk, I'd like to be alone with them."

"I'm so sorry about this."

Jimmy nodded.

On the drive home, Romeo and Juliet curled next to Jimmy, their great heads resting in his lap as if they were both just sleeping. Jimmy ran his fingers through their thick fur and spoke to them in whispers. He told them stories he had heard of dispersers, wolves who left the pack to find new territories; he told them about Sherry and his dreams for the two of them; he told them about his nightmares and how they had come true; he spoke of wild forests in the west and up north where their kind were allowed to live free. He said to them that one day, he and Sherry would live in such a place, a mountain range where there was enough room for people and wolves.

Back at the farm, the truck, with its single headlight, rumbled across the wooden bridge and veered off the driveway past the barn and came to rest in a grassy flat near the creek. Hawk pulled in behind them. Another set of headlights appeared on the drive and crossed the bridge. There was a tense moment until Jimmy realized that it was Woolman's green truck. He pulled to a stop near them. The passenger door opened and Sherry slid out.

She ran to Jimmy, threw her arms around his neck and said, "I made my dad tell me. He wasn't going to until morning. I knew something was wrong. Oh, Jimmy, this is so terrible! I just had to be with you!"

Jimmy held her close. "I'm glad you're here," he said. "I was feeling so alone."

"You're not alone, Jimmy. You're not alone."

"Joe, Lewis, Hawk," Woolman said, "Sorry to intrude like this, but Sherry said she had seen the wolves, too, and she needed to be here. Besides, I wanted to tell you those Tanners are being picked up right now. I asked some state troopers to do that for me. They'll be in the lockup for quite a while."

Lewis said, "Couldn't happen to nicer guys! I'll get the tractor. We'll need the backhoe if there's still some freeze left in the ground. Gotta bury 'em deep so's they don't get disturbed."

Sherry moved to the tailgate and crawled into the truck bed where she knelt between the two bodies. She held her left hand over her mouth to keep from crying out, and, with her right hand, smoothed Juliet's blood stained fur. She looked from one wolf to the other, bowed her head and let the tears flow. Jimmy climbed up beside her and held her heaving shoulders.

"What kind of animal could do such a thing to these beautiful creatures?" she stammered. "Oh, Jimmy, if only we could have saved them, done something. Just one more day and we would have scared them off. Why didn't they leave when those awful men went into the woods after them?"

"I don't know," Jimmy whispered. "I don't know."

Martha walked down to the creek from the house carrying two gray wool blankets. The headlights from the trucks illuminated the burial site. The tractor engine revved as the long arm scooped dirt aside into a mound. Jimmy and Sherry wrapped the wolves in the blankets and lowered them into the dark hole so that they were side by side. Hawk said some words about the Great Circle of Life, shook gourd rattles and sang a chant, which he said would protect the wolves' spirits on their journey. The others took turns dropping clumps of earth into the grave. Then Lewis covered the hole, and they were gone.

For a long while after the others had returned to the house, Jimmy and Sherry stood alone in the dark holding hands, listening to the liquid whispers of Lillibridge Creek flowing full from snowmelt, and, without speaking, thought the same thoughts, saw the same wild visions and felt deeply the same warring emotions which burned within.

23

*W*hen you read the newspapers next week, Mr. Fletcher, you'll know the truth; you'll know that what I wrote in this journal was not the fiction I claimed it to be. Please accept my apologies. I felt that it was important to keep the wolves a secret. I think if I had not lied, they would not have survived as long as they did. I have a feeling though that you knew all along. Thank you for keeping my secret. I am only sorry that it wasn't enough to protect them.

It has only been a few hours since we buried Romeo and Juliet. I can't sleep. There are so many complicated feelings shouting in my head. My heart is full of sorrow, anger, disappointment, grief and loneliness. When I was in the presence of those two wolves at the rendezvous site, all my doubts about the survival of the planet were erased. They represented hope. They were a symbol to me of a world regaining its health. They were beauty and grace. Hawk says that what we witness, we become. Their stealth, loyalty, alertness, stamina and wild hearts now make up part of who I am.

I wish though that I had a switch somewhere to shut off the terrible film loop that plays over and over in my head. There is no sound

track, only the springing of the steel toothed traps and the jolt of wolf
bodies at the impact of bullets. Each time the loop ends, there is a long
silence and a blank screen in my head. It is then that I wonder if each
wolf thought of the other during those last moments, if they had any
idea of death. How in the wolf language would such an idea materialize
in their brain?

My father says it's silly to give animals human capabilities, and I
agree. Even Hawk agrees, but then he always leaves things open. He
said, "Your father is right, but in order to mate for life, I think a wolf
must have some idea of love. And if he is capable of one idea, why not
another."

Hawk also said that the clear pictures in my head will fade, that
my heart will heal, and that I will remember the gifts the wolves gave
me much longer than I will the evil that snuffed them out. He said if
that were not the case, the world would have died of sorrow thousands
of years ago. He's been right about so many things. I hope he is right
about this.

24

Martha did not wake Jimmy until noon. He looked ragged, worn out from wrestling with ghosts in dreams that seemed so real that when he first opened his eyes, he did so tentatively as if he was afraid that his own bedroom with its collection of bird nests, snake skins, crow feathers and wolf photographs was the setting for still another nightmare. The real world flooded him with fresh memories from the night before which were as heart wrenching as the bad dreams had been.

"Jimmy, the day's half gone," his mother said softly. "You should really get up now. Did I mention that Sherry's here?"

"What? Here?" Jimmy leaped from his bed. "How long?"

"Her father just dropped her off. Hawk called Fred early this morning. He suggested that Sherry might like to help you build a kind of memorial down by the creek, a kind of a ritual way to say goodbye. A medicine wheel he said. You know what that is?"

"Ya, sure," Jimmy said pulling on his clothes. He glanced in the mirror. "Oh, lord, I look terrible."

"I don't think Sherry will notice. Your dad is over near Roulette today laying out a foundation for a new house, but he said you could use the stone pile behind the barn. Remember picking those rocks out of the cornfield last spring? There should be plenty. Lewis left the tractor out so you two could use the front loader to move the stone to the creek."

Jimmy grabbed his journal and flew down the stairs. Sherry was sitting at the kitchen table, her hair in a ponytail, her eyes bright. She rose smiling as Jimmy entered.

"Sherry! How can you look so good this early in the morning?"

She took him into her arms and gave him a kiss. "It's afternoon, silly."

"Sorry. I look a mess."

"You look pretty sexy to me."

"Shh! My mother's right in the next room. Are you up to moving some rocks? It's hard work."

"I'm ready. I just need gloves. Your mom said you had extra."

They went out onto the side porch where Jimmy lifted the lid of a built in bench and removed two pairs of work gloves with rough leather palms and fingers. He handed the smaller pair to Sherry.

Martha spoke through the screen door, "I'll bring some sandwiches down in a little bit. Some ice tea, too."

"Where's Hawk, mom? Is he going to help?"

"No. He rode out on Old Star this morning. Said he'd be back tomorrow morning. Needed to spend a night in the woods, I guess. He said when he got back he'd like to take you both for a horseback ride up to the wolf site if you were up to it." Martha dried a breakfast plate with her apron. "You can decide that later. Run along now."

"Thanks, mom."

Jimmy and Sherry walked arm in arm off toward the barn. The sky was a brilliant blue. The fields stretched brown up to the tree line. Hardwoods along the hillside were gray tinged with a hint of green, new buds. Cedar waxwings swooped over the fields cutting through an early hatch. A redwing blackbird whistled down by the creek.

"Are you okay, Jimmy?" Sherry asked as they rounded the corner of the barn.

"Not really," Jimmy said. "It's going to take a while for me to understand why this happened. Every time I picture Romeo and Juliet, I feel like crying."

"That's okay. You're supposed to feel like that. If you didn't there'd be something wrong. If you hold everything in, it might build up until you explode. I wouldn't like that. How would I put you back together again?"

Jimmy smiled and gave her a long hug. He climbed onto the red tractor, which growled to life, and moved it into position near the rock pile. Exhaust billowed from its stack. They loaded the bucket with rocks and rode together down to the creek, the tractor engine groaning under the load.

Jimmy opened his journal and turned to the entry about the medicine wheel Hawk had visited out west. As best he could, Jimmy had sketched the wheel from Hawk's description. He pointed to the drawing and said, "That's what we're going to build. See that? It's a fire ring north of the wheel. We'll do that first and get a fire going."

As they emptied the bucket, flat rocks were set aside for the cairns and cobbles were arranged in a circle. They gathered dead wood from along the creek bank. Jimmy made a bed of dry grass and leaves over which he placed fine twigs and sticks. Sherry lit the fire, which crackled to life as she added larger branches. Gray wood smoke swirled around them and was drawn by a slight wind across the fields to the woods.

They began by building a large central cairn, a rock beehive a yard high and several yards across situated at the head of Romeo and Juliet's grave. A small hole was left in the center, which would be used later. Several more trips were made to the rock pile. Jimmy measured twenty paces from the center north, south, east and west marking each with a flat rock. Smaller cairns were built at each compass point. These outer cairns were joined together by a curved row of rocks, both flat and cobble, all of which formed a great circle, the rim of the wheel. Four stone spokes were laid from the hub out to the four directions. They were just laying the last four spokes when Martha came down from the house carrying a wicker picnic basket.

"My goodness! Look how much you two have done! This is beautiful! You must be starved. Take a break now and eat some egg salad sandwiches and have some tea. Sherry, here's your flute. You said you brought it along to play something when you finished."

"Thanks, Mrs. Warren. I don't know about Jimmy, but I'm hungry as a . . . a . . ." She looked at Jimmy. "I'm very hungry."

Jimmy kept working.

"You stop and eat now, son. You didn't have any breakfast. Hawk said you might need some ribbon or strips of colored cloth so your sisters have been cutting up fabric I had left over from the last quilt. They'll be done soon. We'll all come down then." Martha turned and headed back to the house.

A pair of redtail hawks circled high above the field where Jimmy and Sherry sat eating. The shrill, whistling cries of the two birds cut the silence. Sunlight glinted off their wings each time they banked in an effort to maneuver closer to one another. Their flight was like a slow dance in the great blue dome of the sky.

"They don't know," Jimmy said.

"Know what?" Sherry asked.

"They don't know what's happened here. They don't know about Romeo and Juliet."

"That's true, Jimmy. It's hard to believe that the world just goes on. I'm sure they've known hardship in their lives, lean winters, lost babies. Right now, though, I think they're in love and nothing else exists for them but each other." She nestled against his shoulder.

"The wolves were like that, too."

"I know." Then after a long silence she said, "Why don't we get back to work. There's not much left to do and not a lot of daylight to do it in."

Sherry piled more wood on the fire, pulled on her gloves and picked up a large, rectangular rock, dark gray with veins of black throughout. Jimmy rose slowly and joined her.

Four more spokes were laid to complete the wheel. Jimmy drove the tractor up to the barn and walked back to the creek. Sherry had collected more firewood and built up the fire. Maureen and Sally walked down from the house with Martha, their arms full of multicolored strips of cloth.

Little Sally said, "Jimmy, we're sorry about your wolfs. Maureen an' me made ribbons for you, but where we gonna tie 'em?"

"I've got twine, Jimmy," Martha said.

"What about a flagpole?" Maureen said.

"That's a good idea, sis. I left a hole in the middle for one, but we should put some others around the rim. Mom, could you get my walking stick from the living room? I've got some long poles in the barn that'll work."

Using a sledgehammer while standing on a ladder, Jimmy drove the ten-foot poles deep into the ground at the four outer cairns. He hammered wedges in at the base of the poles to secure them. Twine was strung from the top to the bottom of each pole. Using the stepladder, the girls tied strips of cloth to the twine.

Martha returned with the carved walking stick, a creation of Jimmy's, which Sherry had not seen before.

"You did all that carving yourself?"

"Yea, I just finished it a week ago. This is Romeo howling on top. There by the tree is Juliet. Here's Two Mile Creek flowing away from the rendezvous site. This is the campfire near the laurel and pines. Those two figures by the fire are supposed to be you and me, but we didn't turn out so good. I did that before we started going out." Sherry looked up into his eyes obviously moved. "Down here is the sun setting over the mountains and, on the back, right here is the moon rising. It's Romeo and Juliet's story."

"It's your story, too, Jimmy"

"Our story," he said.

Jimmy attached a piece of twine to the staff and stuck it in the hole in the middle of the stone hub of the wheel. Smaller stones were packed into the hole to steady the stick. As he watched, Maureen and Sally tied cloth strips to it. Finally, Sherry removed the leather necklace Jimmy had given her at the wolf site and tied it to the walking stick. The black and white stones hung between the wolves and the two figures by the campfire.

"I hope you don't mind, Jimmy," she said. "Hawk said you should leave as a tribute something you really valued. The necklace is the most important thing I own."

Jimmy went to her and held her for a long moment. "Will you play something on your flute?"

"Yes," she said.

His mother, sisters and Jimmy sat on the ground each at one of the cairns in the rim of the wheel. Sherry stood near the center with wood smoke swirling around her. The sun was already in the trees along the ridge of the mountain whose shadow slowly flowed into the valley. The air had cooled considerably. The fire crackled and sparked red and gold. The yellow, blue and green ribbons of cloth were brought to life by the evening breeze so that their fluttering sounded like a flock of birds lifting from the field on their way to roost.

Sherry pressed the silver pipe of the flute to her lips and began. Her fingers moved along the keys as if they knew the song well. At first the low notes wove themselves among the natural sounds of wind and fire. One by one they rose like steps up to the sky drawing out to a fine point, a needle to the heart, taking with them the spirits of Romeo and Juliet. There was in this music a mix of sorrow and joy, of loss and hope, all the complicated feelings that flood the body when the heart is broken.

As Sherry eased back down to the long low notes, a hollow tremolo of mourning, Jimmy recognized the howl that he had longed to hear again. His vision was of the two wolves sitting near laurel and pine, heads back, singing their wilderness duet. When she finished and looked at Jimmy, she could see the fire reflected in wet streams down his cheek. She sat beside him and held him close to her. They all remained at their place in the circle until the fire died down and went out.

25

Not all wolf information on the web is positive, Mr. Fletcher. I read about two wolves from a Yellowstone pack that wondered out of the park area a little way into Montana. Both were shot. One died instantly; the other took several weeks to succumb. Sometimes, it was said, animals recover from traumatic injuries on their own. That was not the case for this wolf. When caught, the shooter said he thought they were coyotes. Coyotes are half the size of full-grown wolves. What was he doing shooting coyotes anyway?

Sometimes, those who kill wolves are ranchers or farmers who are afraid of wolf predation. My allowance is small, but I send most of it to a fund set up to compensate those who lose livestock to wolves. Wolf kills on farmland have been just a fraction of what was anticipated when gray wolves were reintroduced in Wyoming. They obviously prefer wild prey. With the fund in place, there is no reason to pull the trigger. Yet shots are still being fired.

According to other web news, poison is still being used. The bodies of two wolves were just discovered near Salmon, Idaho. They had ingested rat poison that causes seizures and convulsions for up to half a day before the heart gives out. How can there be so many Tanners in the world?

So, even though wolves are protected by federal laws, they remain persecuted by man. I hope they get the guys who killed the Idaho wolves. Maybe if enough poachers are prosecuted, they'll get the picture. In order for the Nez Perce Indians in Idaho to keep their adopted Sawtooth pack safe, they'd have to stay with them all the time. That can't be done. Even if it were possible, the wolves would no longer be wild. There are many packs in Idaho now. The federal government has to enforce protection laws. Hawk says that all convicted poachers should be turned over to the Nez Perce who have ways to educate those who find it difficult to show respect for sacred things.

Many of the Mexican wolves recently released in Arizona were killed: shot or poisoned. A large black wolf was shot in the north woods of Maine having migrated there from Canada. Some states are lobbying the federal government to delist the wolf, to remove it from the protection of the Endangered Species Act. Wolf hunting from planes in Alaska has resumed. A single gray wolf that had wondered into Oregon was removed.

While all of this paints a bleak picture for the wolf, fortunately, there are many who are fighting private and public battles on his behalf. Lewis told me earlier tonight that there are people here in this valley who feel as though they have been robbed of the chance of seeing Romeo and Juliet running along Two Mile Creek. They've asked the local judge to throw the book at the Tanners. According to the web, rewards have been posted by environmental groups for information leading to the arrest and conviction of those who kill wolves. Some ranchers and farmers have declared their properties 'predator friendly' so that wolves that live there are never in harms way. They use llamas and guard dogs to discourage wolves from taking livestock. That makes so much sense to me. There are individual landowners in the Adirondacks of New York, the Green Mountains of Vermont, and the White Mountains of New Hampshire who are willing to allow wolves to be released on their property as soon as all the legal and political hurdles are overcome.

If only Romeo and Juliet had found one of those islands of safety. But it is too late for them. From my bedroom window I can see the dark beyond the barn that holds their grave. My anger rises, subsides, then rises again like a recurring fever. There is so much I don't understand. How long will it take for mankind to evolve to the point where he realizes that we need to put the planet right? It has taken several hundred years just to get to the edge of that realization. Maybe Hawk and I will be counted among those who guide us the rest of the way.

26

As he had promised, Hawk was back by Sunday morning. When he rode out of the woods on Old Star, Jimmy and Sherry were standing next to their saddled horses near the medicine wheel. The big, gray horse halted next to them. Hawk dismounted, walked slowly left around the medicine wheel and back to Old Star. From his saddlebags he took a deer antler. The base and two of the lower tines were wrapped with leather straps strung with stone beads. Each of the upper three tines had a hawk feather attached by coarse colored thread. He tied the antler to the carved walking stick.

"It's an excellent wheel. You honor those wolves by giving them such a fine send off on their long journey back to their fathers. We will do more for them when we get back on the mountain. There are parts of the Circle you haven't explored yet. It is those parts we'll discover today if you are ready."

"What are you talking about, Hawk?" asked Jimmy.

"You'll see soon enough. Just follow me and try not to fall off those horses."

Hawk mounted up, turned Old Star and headed across the field. Jimmy helped Sherry get up on the brown and white pinto. He swung up onto the chestnut. They kicked the horses into a gallop chasing after Hawk.

The trail they followed was the same one they had taken the night of the snowstorm. It meandered through the woods near the creek, at first, then cut steeply up the hillside to the flat crest. With each stride Jimmy could see Hawk's long, gray braid whip from side to side. He noticed, too, that Sherry's ponytail bounced in rhythm to her horse's tail. Hooves thudded on firm ground and thumped against fallen logs. The leather saddles creaked as they made their way along the ridge.

The woods was alive with deer, squirrels and birds. Everything scattered as the trio trooped on through stands of budding hardwood, thick walls of pine and tangles of stiff mountain laurel. Jimmy read the signs automatically: tracks in the soft earth, browsed twigs, nut shells strewn at the base of a tree, new clumps of dry grass woven into a cup around the forked branches of a maple, fresh holes pecked square and deep into the side of a dead trunk. Shafts of sunlight filled the woods like glowing blades. The air was wet and fresh. Jimmy breathed deeply and sighed in an attempt to calm himself.

Deep in the woods the trail split. To the right was the rendezvous site. Hawk turned Old Star left.

"Hey, Hawk," Jimmy called out, "you're going the wrong way!"

Hawk turned in his saddle and said, "Remember, when you follow the circle, always go left. Thinking in straight lines only leads to confusion and madness." He laughed his deep laugh and continued left. Sherry smiled back at Jimmy who shrugged his shoulders in defeat and followed.

They rode along the spine of the mountain to the Springs where the trail bent north toward the Rocks. Jimmy knew that this was the perimeter of Romeo and Juliet's territory, the boundary he and Hawk had hiked several months before. Once again memories returned. They were so vivid that he expected at any moment to see the black wolf and his white mate trotting along beside them. His heart grew heavy with the realization that that could not be, that what they were really riding through was an empty woods.

As they approached the Rocks, Jimmy was surprised to see snow.

It was still winter here. Hawk moved left around the back of Giant
Rock, a granite boulder the size of a house, its gray sides covered with
bright green moss and a tangle of exposed roots and vines. Finally,
Hawk dismounted and wrapped Old Star's reins around a low branch.
Sherry and Jimmy did the same.

"I thought we might stop and sit a spell. Sherry, you ever been up
here before?"

"When I was little. I remember Bird Rock there and, of course,
Dead Man's Cave. I was always too scared to go in."

There was some flat ground between Giant and Bird Rocks where
a fire ring had been built years ago. The snow around it was gone.
Jimmy held his hand over the black coals and charred stones.

"Someone had a fire here recently. There's still heat coming out of
the rocks. And look at all these tracks. A man was here and look at that
over there," Jimmy said.

Hawk smiled. "Bear. He surprised me last night, but I managed to
chase him off. Spring bears are hungry."

"This is where you spent the night?" Sherry asked.

"Yes."

"Alone?"

"Not quite. There was the bear."

Jimmy smiled at Sherry's startled look. She continued, "Why did
you come all the way up here?"

"I came to listen."

"Listen?"

"Yes. You learn more that way. Why don't we try it for a little
while."

"Hawk," said Jimmy, "did you block the cave entrance with those
branches?"

"I didn't want the bear to move in while I was gone. Let's sit."

Jimmy brushed some wet snow from a low rock and offered the
seat to Sherry. He and Hawk sat in the snow. Above them loomed the
great slab of granite, Giant Rock, covered with lichen like peeling,
green skin. In its cracks and crevices small islands of green moss clung.
At its base was the brush pile that hid the mouth of Dead Man's Cave.

They listened. The horses shuffled and snorted. A jay and some chicka-dees called from small trees growing out of the tops of the rocks. The distant drumming of a woodpecker vibrated in a ravine further down the ridge.

"Hawk," Sherry whispered, "how did the cave get its name?"

"As I heard it, it was named back when the town was called Canoe Place. There wasn't much here, just a trading post along the river and us Indians. The river was the highway then. A greedy man who owned a sawmill in the valley said he owned the mountains, too. He came up here to figure out how to cut down all the trees and get them to the river. Trees meant money, the thing he was most interested in. As it turned out, he never returned. Somehow the story got around that he was buried in the floor of the cave. The trees here are so old because people still think he haunts the place. But it's just a story. Probably there's a better one. Now it's time to hear what the Rocks want to tell you. Listen carefully."

The mid-day sun poured light onto Bird Rock so that the tiny flecks of mica imbedded there sparkled like miniature constellations through which ran rivulets of melting snow. Sherry focused on the graceful lines of the bird carved into the rock. Jimmy watched the tree branches tremble in the subtle breeze above. Hawk closed his eyes.

Then it came to the three of them at the same time. Hawk looked up. Jimmy and Sherry looked at each other as if to say 'did you hear that?' So faint a sound like someone calling from a great distance. Then a mewing, closer, high pitched like a tree squeaking. Then again louder, more urgent joined by other voices calling. Jimmy looked at the cave.

"I think it's coming from in there," he said.

"You should look," said Hawk.

"Sherry, help me with this."

They pulled the branches clear exposing the dark mouth of the cave. The walls and ceiling were scorched black by thousands of years of campfires dating back to the first people. The cries emanating from the dark throat of the cave were frantic now. Jimmy ducked his head to avoid hitting the low ceiling and scrambled in.

"What is it, Jimmy? Can you see anything?" Sherry called in after him.

"There are bones all over the place."

"Bones? Human bones?"

"I don't think so. Animal bones, most likely. Just a minute, Sherry. Now I see them. They're way back in here. I don't know if I can reach them. Got one. Two."

Jimmy backed out of the cave. He turned and faced Sherry and Hawk. He held out two gray wolf pups.

"Oh, my! Oh, my! They're adorable, Jimmy," Sherry said taking the pups.

"Hawk," Jimmy said, "you knew they were here didn't you?"

"Yes, but you needed to find them yourself. This is the part of the Circle you haven't walked before."

The pups squirmed and squealed in Sherry's lap, their little, gray bodies shivering.

"Sherry, I can't reach the others. I'm too big to make it all the way back in there."

"Others?"

"There's at least two more. You'll have to get them."

"I don't think so."

"Hawk won't fit. You're the only one who can do it."

Hawk said, "There's nothing to be worried about. The snakes won't wake up for another month maybe, and, according to legend, the dead man is buried too deep for you to bump into his bones."

"Thanks," said Sherry handing the pups to Jimmy.

Hawk pulled a flashlight out of his coat. "This may help."

Reluctantly, Sherry entered the cave. She complained the whole way in about spider webs and dirt, then was silent for some time. She emerged with soot smudged on her cheeks and strands of spider webs in her hair. In her left hand was another gray pup and, in the right, a white one bawling and working the air with all four paws. They were both frantic, eyes wide, fur like fuzz, just weeks old, four or five pounds each.

Hawk brought two canning jars of milk from his saddlebags. "This should calm them down. It's goat milk, but it's all I could get."

"There's still one more in there," said Sherry who disappeared again into the dark cave. There were no complaints this time. Moments later she crawled out smiling. In her hand she held a black wolf pup. Jimmy took him into his arms and stroked the dark fur, petted the tiny head between limp ears and stared into the golden eyes. The black was larger than the rest by several pounds. Compared to his small body, his feet were massive. Jimmy just grinned without saying a word. Sherry sat beside him letting the other pups crawl over her. They mewed and licked her face and hands.

Hawk put a rubber glove on each jar of milk, poked tiny holes in the tips of the fingers and held the jars upside down.

"The pups were born a little early. What we have are three females and two males. The black and the smallest gray there are the males. These orphans certainly can't survive out here on their own. Let's see if they'll take milk. Make sure that glove doesn't slip off. We don't want to drown 'em. I think they're just really surprised to see us rather than their parents. You know, Sherry, Friday night you asked why Romeo and Juliet didn't leave. I came up here yesterday to look for the answer. Now we know they wouldn't have left even if we had tried to scare them away. They might have moved the pups to a new den, but they wouldn't leave them."

All five pups drank greedily. Sherry looked from Jimmy to the pups and back to him. He was beaming.

Hawk said, "I have a plan. It might not work, but at least we can try. You have to be willing to give these guys up though. They need a wild home with other wolves."

Jimmy's face darkened as he looked at Hawk.

"It's the only way for them to survive, Jimmy," Hawk said.

His face softened. "Whatever's best for them, I'll do it."

"The first thing is not to give them names. Let them name themselves. For the plan to work, I'll need both of you to help. You guys don't have school this week, Sherry, so your dad said you could go along with us tomorrow."

"Go along? Where?"

"To the Adirondacks."

"Way up in New York?"

"Those are the closest Adirondacks to us."

Sherry smiled at Hawk and said, "I'd love to go."

"Let's get these babies home. We'll talk over the details tonight." Hawk got burlap sacks out of his saddlebags. Each pup was placed in a bag except for the black. The bags were tied to the saddle horns of Old Star and Sherry's pinto. Jimmy zipped the black into his coat with the tiny head peeking out. They weren't far down the trail before the wolf pup was asleep.

Jimmy and Sherry were watching the pups sleep on the straw floor of the horse stall when Hawk entered the barn. Pigeons stirred and cooed high in the dark rafters. The kerosene lantern cast a weak yellow light on the tractor, bails of hay, rows of pitch forks, shovels, picks, hoes, and rakes, as well as the tangle of leather harnesses which dangled from tarnished brass hooks on the wood plank wall.

"Your father should be here soon, Sherry," said Hawk. "He said he didn't want to know what we were up to, otherwise, as warden, he might have to interfere. So don't talk to him about the pups until after they're released."

Jimmy turned to him. "What's the plan, Hawk?"

"Well, I have this friend, Twin Bears. He's Mohawk. We used to fish and hunt together when we were young during the Gatherings when all the tribes got together. Like me, he refused to live on a reservation. He bought some land near Newcomb on the south slopes of the High Peaks. He kept adding to it over the years. Casinos and the stock market were good to him. He bought a whole valley from the paper company.

"Twin Bears has always been interested in wolves. He wants to see them running wild again in those mountains. When I called him for advice about the pups, he got so excited. He has a mated pair of gray wolves in a five-acre enclosure. He thinks they might act as foster parents for your pups. It's a gamble, though. They'll either accept them or kill them. Some biologists, he told me, tried fostering out west where it worked both ways. The other possibility is that the adults will just ignore them. That would not be good.

"It's your call, Jimmy. If you don't like the plan then we can give the pups to the zoo up in Buffalo. They'd take 'em in a minute."

"These wolves aren't going to spend the rest of their lives in cages. That's not living," Jimmy said. "We don't have a choice. We have to go to the Adirondacks. How will Twin Bears release the wolves?"

"He calls it a 'soft' release. The wolves spend a month or more in the pen so they become accustomed to the forest, the smells, the wind, the sky, the plants, the sound of water. That way, when he lets them go, they may not roam as far. The way he sees it, he's releasing them on his land, but, of course, if they roam further out, which they will, he doesn't feel he's responsible which, of course, he is. Once they're loose in the woods, all seven of them are on their own. They may survive if they avoid hikers and farms, or they may meet the same fate as Romeo and Juliet. It's not easy being a wolf. Twin Bears did say that there is enough room in those mountains for a dozen packs. They'd have more than enough to eat.

"He said even though there's been a lot of talk about reintroducing wolves up there, it's not exactly legal to do it yet. But he told me that laws were made for men, not wolves. He thinks that if our wolves are discovered, people will think they came from Canada. That's already happened in Maine. Twin Bears' wolves did come from the far north, near James Bay, but he went and got them. No one knows his wolves are there. It's his secret. Sound familiar? They're young, but he thinks they'll den up next year. If they take to your pups, they'll get some experience parenting."

"What time do we leave?" Sherry asked.

"It's a half day's drive so we'll be at your place around five. Sounds like your dad pulling in now. I'll tell him you'll be right along."

Sherry opened the stall gate and knelt next to the heap of pups. She petted each one gently stroking their small bodies, their tiny faces, fur as soft as down. They fidgeted in their sleep and caressed each other with paws over eyes and heads on shoulders. Then she stood, put her arms around Jimmy and held him until her father sounded the truck horn.

They had passed Andrews Settlement on Rt. 49 and were near Gold when Hawk looked in the rearview mirror and said, "Sherry, you see that little creek running through the pasture? It's the Allegheny River! This is where it starts, the headwaters. Flows all the way across the state to Pittsburgh where it joins the Monogahela to form the Ohio. I wonder how many people down there have ever visited here. It's good to trace the source of things."

Jimmy whispered from the back seat of the old, silver Subaru wagon, "Hawk, she's asleep. She didn't hear a word you said, but I did."

"Good. I already talk to myself enough as it is. Glad someone is listening." Hawk studied Jimmy in the mirror. "You don't look so good."

"I spent the night in the barn with the pups. I didn't get much sleep."

"Were they restless all night?"

"No, I was. They were up around three. I fed them and they went right back to sleep. They ran around for an hour before you got there so they're worn out again."

Three of the pups were curled in Sherry's lap. She slept with her head on Jimmy's shoulder. The other two pups, a gray and the black, were cradled in Jimmy's arms.

"You better get some sleep. We got us a long ride. We'll pick up Rt. 17 in Corning and head east for a while. We'll take back roads going north through Utica and Old Forge."

Jimmy closed his eyes and did not dream, but fell into a deep sleep where the heart knew neither grief nor joy, only the sweet rest where the continual mutterings of the mind are quieted.

Hawk drove on under a blue marble sky through the old Allegheny Mountains, north into New York State where he passed through Corning, continued on to Binghamton, the western Catskill Mountains, where he proceeded north to Utica, then northeast into the Adirondacks. Just beyond Old Forge, not far from Raquette Lake, he heard the pups stir. He turned off the highway onto a dirt road that lead deep into a pine woods. A quarter mile in was a clearing that had been logged years ago. It was filled with stumps and slash piles. He shifted into four-wheel drive, followed a rutted skidder trail and came to a stop behind an immense pile of brush.

"Everyone out. Break time," he said. "Jimmy, help me get the pen out of the back. We'll let the pups do their business in there rather than in the car. It already smells bad enough in here."

Jimmy put his two pups on Sherry's lap. "You awake?" he said.

"Not quite, but I'll take them. They're so warm. Are we in New York yet?"

Hawk lifted the rusted trunk lid. "We've been in New York for hours. We're almost at the end of our journey. You two were just wore out. We need to feed the pups once more before we get there. I brought along some stuff for us, too."

After the pups were fed, Hawk and Jimmy set the wire cage near the brush pile, lifted the lid and placed the pups inside. They squealed and romped over one another. The black bit at the wire trying to get out.

The three travelers talked quietly while they ate fruit and drank tea. Hawk held up his hand for silence. They thought they could hear a plane coming over the ridge on the far side of the highway. "Get down," Hawk said. "It's a truck coming up the road." They lay on the ground behind the brush pile and listened. The ten wheeler groaned and bellowed black exhaust from chrome stacks as it made its way toward the clearing.

"Did you see those 'no trespassing' signs, Hawk?" Jimmy whispered.

"Yea, but I never pay any attention to them. Every time I get caught I just tell them I'm lost and apologize like crazy. I think it's easier to ask for forgiveness than permission. They fall for it every time. But we don't want anyone to see these pups. That would not be good."

The truck slowed to a crawl as it neared the clearing. The driver downshifted and blew a cloud of black smoke. He revved the engine and accelerated past the clearing and disappeared up the mountainside. For a long time after the truck was gone, they could hear the dying roar of the engine.

"We better get outta here," said Hawk. "Let's get the pups in the car and get going."

They loaded the cage into the way-back and quickly headed down the dirt road toward the highway. Jimmy and Sherry removed the pups from the pen and let them play on their laps. Hawk drove east to Blue Mountain and north to Long Lake. There he turned east again moving deeper into the mountains. They were low like the Alleghenies, but the forest cover here was predominantly pine with clusters of white birch and intermittent stands of hardwoods. Hawk said, "Twin Bears likes this area because there are so many black bears. Once you get to know him, you might think his parents were bears."

A dozen miles east of Long Lake, they stopped at Newcomb. The panoramic scene before them was the vast stretches of the south slopes of the High Peaks, the highest of which was Mt. Marcy. Hawk turned to the back seat and said, "The Algonquin called the big mountain Tahawas, Cloudsplitter. Some say a writer just made up the name. Writers are always doing stuff like that so you don't always know the truth. Sounds like a good name to me. If it wasn't their word, I'll bet money the Algonquin wish they had thought it up first. I wonder how the mountain got along before it had a name? Anyway, it's a little over five thousand feet high. Just up there below the snowline is Lake Tear of the Clouds where another great river begins, the Hudson. That's where we're headed."

Jimmy and Sherry held the pups up so they could see. There were almost a dozen peaks with names, according to the marker before them, like Mt. Skylight, Mt. Marshall, Algonquin, Avalanche, Boundary Peak, Pinnacle, Haystack, Panther Peak, and Couchsachraga, which together created a jagged silhouette against the dark blue sky. At three thousand feet, the snowline was drawn horizontally across the range dividing it into distinct seasons. Spring was along the base. Above, the snow covered peaks looked like a row of canine teeth.

"The pups should go back in the cage. We're almost there. Twin

Bears said there's a macadam road just out of town that'll take us up near his place. If we come to the strip mine, we'll have to back up a mile or so. There's no road into his place, but he said if we honk he'll come out and meet us."

The wolf pups mewed and yipped inside the wire cage. Hawk headed east then turned directly north onto a narrow road, which led along a creek that was halted in its flow by a series of beaver dams. From the flood pools above each dam rose the domed humps of beaver huts. Like carved spikes, the chewed stumps of trees lined the bank. Hawk slowed for a flock of dark colored turkeys crossing the road. Further on, from a small meadow across the creek, a whitetail watched them pass.

They drove deep into the wilderness. The pavement ended. The road narrowed and curved precipitously along the creek bank. Pine boughs smacked the windshield and mud sucked at the wheels. Although it was spring here, the season wasn't as advanced as back home. The air had cooled considerably and traces of snow were evident in the darker shadows of the woods.

Ahead, tacked to the trunk of a towering white pine, was a tan leather shield in the center of which were the yellow silhouettes of a wolf and two bears. Above them, in quick brush strokes were the snowcapped mountains. Hanging above the shield was a deer skull whose antlers spread out like branches. From each of the tines hung strings of beaded rawhide woven around the shafts of dangling eagle feathers, a silent wind chime.

Hawk pulled into a small clearing by the pine. He honked the horn twice and got out. "This is it!" he said. "Let's show those pups their new home."

They carried the cage carefully to the center of the clearing and lowered it into a nest of dead grass. The pups were sniffing the air, squealing and stumbling over one another. Within minutes, Twin Bears was there on a chestnut stallion, leading a string of three other horses and a mule with wicker baskets attached to its sides. Twin Bears wore jeans, a sweatshirt, a dark leather vest and a wide brimmed leather hat. Hanging from his belt was a large hunting knife on the left and, on the right, a Colt pistol in a tooled leather holster. His hair was long, gray and loose like a horse's mane. His handsome, square face was weathered with deep lines that softened when he smiled.

"Hawk, you old bear," Twin Bears said as he dismounted. The two embraced. "It is good to see you, friend. I'm pleased you've come. These two young people must be the ones you spoke of who carry the wolf spirit. My home is honored by your presence." He extended his hand to Sherry who shook his timidly. He held onto her hand and said, "Hawk told me you were as beautiful as a mountain spring. For once, he did not exaggerate."

Sherry blushed.

Hawk said, "Sherry, Jimmy, this is Twin Bears."

Twin Bears shook Jimmy's hand and held it for a minute. "There are those among my people who say that in some men the wolf blood flows strong. If all that Hawk has told me is true, you are one of those human beings."

Hawk said, "You know I only speak the truth."

"This is so, my friend, but you have been known to subscribe to two truths. One is the truth of the world we all see and the other is the truth only *you* see in your imagination."

Hawk smiled. "Is my imagination so strong that it can create a litter of wolf pups?" He pointed his open hand toward the pen.

Twin Bears knelt in the grass beside the wire cage. He moved his clasped hands over it to indicate the four directions. Then, hands open, palms down, he moved them in a clockwise circle four times. His hands rested on the lid. The wolf pups seemed hypnotized at first, and then stretched up to lick his fingers. "Welcome, wild ones. No one will harm you here." He turned to Hawk. "We should go. Sometimes hikers use this road. We don't want to draw a crowd. My place is just a few miles in."

"A few miles? How'd you get here so fast?" Hawk asked.

"I could hear you banging up the road in that old car."

"Well, it runs. You don't even have a car."

"I don't even have a road. Let's go. We can put the pups in the baskets."

"I'd like to carry the black, if you don't mind, Twin Bears. And Sherry wants to take the white. We'll zip them into our coats."

"That is as it should be. That way, when you return home, you'll have the memory of their heartbeats next to you and they will have yours with them. We should go."

The trail zigzagged along a creek crossing it many times. There were rushing waterfalls all silvery and jeweled that spilled into deep, green plunge pools. Except for the trail, the forest seemed impenetrable with crowded dark pines and thick underbrush. Eventually the riders came into a large stand of white birch that was more open and filled with shafts of sunlight. The vertical, white trunks gave way to an open meadow divided down the center by the creek they had been following. At the far end of the meadow stood a low, honey colored log cabin with smoke rising from a stone chimney. On the sloped roof were four solar panels and a small satellite dish. Turning a wooden wheel to the left of the cabin was a high waterfall. The wheel shaft disappeared into a wooden shed. Behind the house the mountain rose dramatically. Exposed rock and leaning pines seemed to hang over the building.

Twin Bears led the troop across the field past the horse barn. From its corner extended a high chain link fence, which looked as if it were meant to keep deer out of a garden, but was actually designed to keep wolves in. They halted by a hitching rail and dismounted. Twin Bears spoke to Jimmy and Sherry, "You should say your goodbyes to the pups now. I've built a pen inside the main enclosure. We'll put them in there. If my wolves act hostile toward the pups, they wont be able to get at them. If that is the outcome, we'll have to find another home for the pups. At least they wont be killed. You probably worried about that."

"How will you know if they are accepted by the adults?" Jimmy asked.

"They'll tell us. When we know, we just pull the rope, the cage door opens and all will be well. If it goes that way, we'll keep them together for two more weeks. I've built a gate at the back of the enclosure that will swing open when it's time. You'll have to come back for the release. It'll be quite a moment, seven wolves in the High Peaks."

Hawk got two of the gray pups from one basket and Twin Bears got the others. They tried feeding them once more, but the pups were too excited to drink. Jimmy, Sherry and Hawk followed Twin Bears into the enclosure. All five pups were placed in a wire box several yards square. Within was a trough of water and a wooden bench for shelter.

The pups pranced around tripping on irregular ground and each other. One of the grays sat in the water trough and yawned. The white explored the shade of the bench and fell asleep there. Soon all three grays joined her, their eyes disappearing under heavy lids. The black sat in a far corner, sniffed the air and stared up into the woods a hundred yards away.

"Where are your wolves?" Sherry asked.

"They're people shy which is good. You can bet they know we're here. They'll both stay up in the woods until no one's around. They've only been here about three weeks so they're still getting used to the place."

"What color are they?" asked Jimmy.

"You'll see. We can go up on the porch, have a bite to eat and keep watch with binoculars and my old spotting scope. The sooner we get out of here, the better."

The sun moved across the meadow. Hawk fell asleep in the rocker with a quilt over his lap. Jimmy and Sherry sat on a bench sipping hot tea. They took turns telling Twin Bears the story of Romeo and Juliet. Jimmy showed him his journal. When they finished, he told them stories, bear stories, wolf stories. He was nearly finished telling them about his first sighting of a wolf in Denali when he stopped mid-sentence.

"There they are!" he said pointing toward the woods. "Look through the scope, Jimmy. Be quiet, though, no sudden moves or they'll disappear."

"Oh, yes," Jimmy said making fine adjustments to focus the lens. "They're half way to the cage. Both grays. One is huge!"

Twin Bears handed Sherry a pair of binoculars and whispered, "The male is about a hundred twenty pounds. The female, around eighty-five or ninety. They've been eating well here. I've been bringing road killed deer, rabbits, a fisher, and some raccoons. Also, I've done a little hunting for them. Eating is a good sign. It means they aren't too stressed."

Sherry shook Hawk awake and handed him the binoculars. "You've got to see this, Hawk."

He blinked, rubbed his eyes and peered through the lenses. "I was dreaming of a young girl I knew once. I think she would have come to my cabin if you hadn't gotten me up. She was very beautiful."

Twin Bears said, "There he goes again, living in his imagination. You have better luck with women there, my friend, than here."

"Sorry, Hawk," said Sherry.

"It's okay. I know where she lives. Right now I'm looking at wolves. These two are beauties. They seem curious enough. Have they been growling?"

"Not yet," said Jimmy. "Let's see what they do?"

The grays moved slowly through the high tangle of brown grass toward the pen where the pups slept. Even the black was sleeping. The adults walked close together, sniffed the air reading the new odors that lingered there. They kept their narrow, yellow eyes riveted to the cage. The male was dark gray with a white belly and legs. The rough mane of fur, which puffed around its neck, was a mottled mix of white and gray. The female was almost the same except her face was much lighter. Each held its black tipped tail straight out.

As they neared the pen, the pair split and circled it in opposite directions. The pups began to stir and sniff. The black sprung to his feet and yapped. Both adults leapt back and stared. The others emerged from under the bench and stood blinking in the strong sunlight. They began jumping one another and playing in the water trough oblivious to the presence of the adults. It was several minutes before they all gathered around the black and stood silently staring at the two pairs of yellow eyes watching them. There was a long silence. One of the gray pups moved to the wire mesh and yapped. Except for the black, the others did the same.

The adults began circling the cage once again close enough that their great shadows passed over the pups. They paced around the pen a dozen times, sniffing with lowered heads. The pups followed them bumping into one another. The black sat still in the middle.

The large male moved off toward the woods and lay down near a tree stump. The female watched him go. She circled the pen several more times then laid down with her back against the wire mesh. The pups squealed and leapt against her. She stretched out full length and yawned. The big gray returned to the pen, sniffed its full perimeter and stood next to his mate. She licked his leg, he her ears. The little black watched.

"Will you look at that," Jimmy whispered. "I never thought about the possibility of one of the pups not accepting the adults. Your wolves don't seem hostile at all, Twin Bears."

"Keep watching. We need to know that they don't think these pups are food."

"What's the black doing?" whispered Sherry to Jimmy.

"Just sitting there."

Hawk said, "He's thinking. They are all communicating like crazy, but not in a language we know. Things don't smell quite right to the black. Give him a little more time."

The big gray finally lay down next to his mate, his great head erect, alert; eyes focused on the black. After a long moment, the black looked away, got up and trotted over to the trough where he drank. He whirled around, ran to the other pups and leapt on them. They were a tumbling ball of yaps and squeals. When they untangled themselves, each pressed against the wire mesh in order to touch the reclining female, the black included. The female licked at their faces through the wire.

"Did you see that, Jimmy?" said Sherry.

"Yes. That's the signal you were talking about, Twin Bears, isn't it?"

"That's the one. I think this is going to work."

"How soon can we open the pen?"

"They've told us what we needed to know. Why don't you pull that rope, Jimmy. We can open the gate right from here."

Jimmy pulled the rope taut. The pen door flipped open. Both adults leapt up and skittered several yards towards the woods. The pups seemed bewildered. They stood looking at each other. Then the black walked toward the opening with the white right behind him. Once they cleared the gate, the three gray pups followed. They ran to the adults who sniffed and nudged each one. The female began licking four of the pups. The adult male stood still as if posing while the small black stood under him peering out at the others through long legs.

27

wj 6 May

Somewhere I read that in the Hoh Rainforest on the Olympic Peninsula of Washington state there are giant chestnut trees hundreds of feet tall. When one topples over it becomes a nursery log from which new trees grow. The young trees draw nourishment from the fallen tree through thick roots that cover it like vines. As the young trees mature, the nursery log becomes earth again. The roots continue to arch over the fallen tree as if it were still there. It's possible, I've heard, for a man to walk under the new trees like walking through a tunnel.

Salmon live for years in the ocean. When it is time, they struggle for many miles up the stream of their birth until they reach the spawning ground. The females lay their pearl eggs amongst the stones that line the riverbed. The male fertilizes the eggs. Then they both die.

Life and death and life. Good and evil. Love and hate. Calm and chaos. A cycle, round and round. This is how it is for all living things, even wolves. Although my heart is heavy, at least I understand the gift I was given by Romeo and Juliet. They taught me to see the beauty in the world by being beautiful. From them I learned that nature is not capable of evil, that life depends on death and that death is part of the Circle we all travel. Those two wolves gave me a glimpse of how the world could be.

Hawk says that if you want to live on a planet that makes room for bear, mountain lion, wolf, you must first create that world in your imagination, in your dreams, before such a world can become real. I have done that.

When I told you about finding the wolf pups, you seemed very excited. Mr. Fletcher, I wish you could have been there last week in the Adirondacks. You would have had a lifetime of fuel for those poems you write. My dad, Hawk and Sherry Woolman were with me. We had camped in Twin Bears' meadow Friday night lulled to sleep by the waterfall. Before sunup, he and Hawk had a roaring bonfire going. Neither of them are young men, but they danced barefoot for hours, their beaded leather necklaces and hair feathers bouncing in the firelight. The chant they sang was in a language I did not know, but somehow understood. The rest of us took turns beating on a drum, hide stretched over a length of hollow log. We kept a steady rhythm which Hawk said would help us meditate, visualize the wolf pack working their way deep into the High Peaks, their new world.

It was a ceremony to honor the rising sun, the new day, all of the things of the forest, asking them to receive the seven wolves we were about to release. Once the day was 'fully born' as Twin Bears called it, we hiked up into the woods to the north end of the enclosure. There, Twin Bears and Hawk had built tree stands for each of us so that we would not spook the wolves. When we were all perched high above the chain link fence, I pulled a rope that lifted the latch and swung the gate open.

We waited. Twin Bears had placed a deer carcass a mile up the mountainside to lure the wolves out of the pen. We were there more than an hour before we saw the first wolf. It was the adult female. Trailing behind her were three pups, the white and two grays. I was amazed at how much they had grown. It seemed they had doubled in size in just a few weeks. The female stopped at the open gate suspiciously sniffing the air. The pups bounded right through barking and jumping one another. The female followed.

A few minutes later the third gray pup emerged from the thick laurel followed by the adult male. Neither paused at the gate, but ran through right under us. They grouped together about twenty-five yards from the fence. The adults looked back in our direction waiting for the black pup to appear. When he did not show, the large male began to howl, long, low notes like the ones that came from Sherry's flute. Immediately the female joined in, as did the four pups with their short yaps. The chorus sent chills down my spine. I could feel my heart thumping.

A high-pitched cry came from the laurel. Then the black pup scrambled out of the brush. I was even more startled at how big he had gotten. He was twice the size of the other pups and more agile. He joined the pack, which moved slowly along a dry creek bed up the hillside until they were out of sight.

The whole thing seems like a story someone would make up. But it isn't. There are wolves roaming those mountains. They are marking their territory, hunting in the dark valleys, drinking from hidden lakes and sleeping in caves that have no names. I hope other people have it in their imaginations to keep them from harm. Hope is a powerful gift, Hawk says, like a flower that blooms from ash after the earth has been scorched by fire. I know now that he is right.

I am writing this last entry sitting on Giant Rock high above Dead Man's Cave. Below is our campfire where Sherry sits writing down her own thoughts. We have trusted each other with our secret lives. I think that the book we write together will be a long one.

Looking west from here across the tops of the endless mountains, I see the red sun sliding down to the other side of the world. Looking east, the moon, round and pale, rises above the plateau like the yellow eye of a wolf on its nightly hunt following a well-worn trail across the sky as if nothing has happened. In truth, everything has happened.

Wolf Journal by Brian A. Connolly

The young adult novel adults should read!

Further Wolf Reading:

- www.totalyellowstonepage.com, John Uhler
- www.wolf.org, International Wolf Center, Ely, Minnesota
- www.defenders.org, Defenders of Wildlife
- www.wolfhaven.org, Washington
- www.wolfcenter.org, Idaho
- www.forwolves.org, Idaho
- www.wolftracker.com, Yellowstone

- *A Sand County Almanac*, Aldo Leopold, Oxford University Press, 1949.
- *The Wolf: The Ecology and Behavior of an Endangered Species*, L. David Mech, Ian McTaggart, University of Minnesota Press, 1985.
- *The Wolves of Denali*, L. David Mech, Layne Adams, Thomas Meier, John Burch, and Bruce Dale, University of Minnesota Press, 1998.
- *Out Among the Wolves: Contemporary Writings on the Wolf*, Edited by John A. Murray, Whitecap Books, 1993.
- *Of Wolves and Men*, Barry Lopez, Simon & Schuster, 1978.
- *Discovering Yellowstone Wolves*, James Halfpenny and Diann Thompson, published by A Naturalist's World, Gardiner, Montana, 1996.
- *Ecological Studies of Wolves on Isle Royale*, Annual Report, Rolf O. Peterson, 1996-1997. (pamphlet)

Printed in the United States
3396

9 781401 038632